BLURB

ALLY DOESN'T WANT TO HAVE ANYTHING TO DO WITH werewolves. Kade is a werewolf who wants to *do* everything to Ally.

Just because Ally Rose can turn into a wolf, doesn't mean that she's happy about her status as a shape-shifting, occasionally howling, never-butt-sniffing werewolf. As a result, she has only two rules in life: 1) avoid werewolf packs at all costs and 2) stay the hell away from the man who turned her against her will. Packs are evil...violent... deadly... And the wolf who turned her is the worst of the worst.

Just because Kade Blackwood is the Alpha's brother, doesn't mean he can ignore a direct order — even when it's something as mundane as packing up an old woman's belongings and hauling them back to the pack house in Ashwood. But all of his good intentions fly out of the window the moment he steps foot in tiny Pepper, Georgia…and smells *her*. His mate.

He wants her. Craves her. Aches for her. But first he has to find her…before the wolf hunting Ally gets his paws on her.

REAL MEN SNARL

REAL MEN SHIFT

CELIA KYLE

MARINA MADDIX

REAL MEN
RMANCE

CHAPTER ONE

ONE FALSE STEP AND ALLY ROSE WOULD BE DOWN FOR THE count. Strips of woven nylon wrapped around her legs, randomly tightening and then loosening. It was only a matter of time before she hit the pavement.

Well, pavement and probably a dog or two.

Six dog leashes twined around her legs while the mutts on the other end sniffed and barked and pooped. *Everywhere.* Then they had to pee on the exact same spot as one of the others or the world would *end.*

When Bernstein, a fluffy white Pomeranian with the personality of a bull mastiff, weaved between her open legs, then jumped and tried to lick her hand, Ally decided enough was enough.

The pups grumbled and whined but a few creative lunges, a handful of ducks, and one twist into a pretzel and she was finally free. The dogs looked up at her, panting happily, as if her bid for freedom had been a fun game.

She crouched low—not an easy task for a big girl who stood five-foot-nine—and allowed each one to give her a slobbery doggy kiss. She ignored the passersby, pretending she didn't have an audience while she allowed herself to be licked to death by a pack of over groomed furballs.

"Okay kiddos," she raised her voice above the barks and yips as she stood, "time to head back."

Like everything else during their walk, turning around and going home wasn't that simple. She reached down to pat Jake the bulldog on the head, which was when Bernstein decided to tug on his leash and make a break for it. And he did, the little ball of adorable pain-in-the-assness.

The silly fluffball sprinted headlong into the street, and Ally's heartbeat picked up its pace, thumping fast and hard. His pink leash bounced along the ground behind him, a bright spot of color against the dark asphalt.

A quick glance down the empty street reassured her that Bernstein wasn't about to become hamburger, and she breathed a little easier. This wasn't the first time in the last few years that she was thankful she'd moved to sleepy Pepper, Georgia.

Ally glanced around once more, this time for anyone who

might hear what she was about to do. She was fine with her reputation as an anti-social hermit, but she didn't want to add 'crazy lady who thinks she's a wolf' to the list. Crouching low, she allowed her inner wolf to come forward. Its rumbling, feral growl had brought more than one uppity pooch back in line over the years, and it didn't fail with Bernstein.

The little Pom skidded to a stop, turned on his heel, and scampered back to her, head low and tail between his legs. He laid down at her feet, whimpering his puppy apology. Ally's heart surged with affection for the little rebel and rubbed his head to show there were no hard feelings.

"Aw, sweetheart," she murmured. "It's okay," she whispered as she scooped him up with one hand. "You have to be more careful. You could have been flattened."

He took her reassurance as praise and nearly wriggled right out of her arms as he showed his happiness. Still wiggling that little tail, he gave her a very wet, and more than a little disgusting, face bath with his tongue. She groaned and tipped her head back, trying to stay out of reach and keep an eye on the others, but Bernstein was a persistent little shit. She rounded the next corner and passed a tall man in a baseball cap. She pasted on her normal, polite smile as she and her unruly pack scampered past.

"Looks like you have your hands full." He seemed friendly enough, but Ally kept her eyes averted.

She nodded, then hurried on without a word, as she always did. She loved walking the dogs, but they were people magnets. Unfortunately, Ally most definitely *wasn't* a people person. At all. Sure, once upon a time, but... Life had kicked her in the teeth and taught her to keep to herself. It was safer that way.

Two blocks down and one block over on Front Street was their destination—the town's small veterinary practice. Getting them inside the building and into the back area with the kennels took almost as much time as their actual walk. Between the wiggling, the yapping, and flat-out barking, she hardly managed to get everyone behind the swinging door.

Every walk ended with a treat, and they wanted theirs *now!*

Mia, a young, African American vet tech, took the leads from Ally and helped her tuck each pup back into its assigned cage. "Did they all behave?" She glanced up from behind pretty purple and black twists.

"For the most part," Ally popped Bernstein into his cage, "except for this little monster. Tried to make a break for it, right into the street."

Mia laughed and shook her head, curls swinging with the movement. "That's a man for you. Never knows what a good thing he has till it's gone."

Ally smiled awkwardly as Mia chuckled and finished up

with the dogs, fighting the urge to laugh along with Mia. She liked everyone at the vet's office well enough, but her policy of keeping humans at arm's length included her coworkers, as well. She'd only allowed herself the luxury of becoming close with two humans, and that was simply because they wouldn't accept anything less.

"Lucy coming home soon?" Mia asked. "Tessa must be going cray-cray."

When Ally's best friend from college, Lucy Morgan, had decided to reconnect with her roots in Ashtown, a couple hours away, she'd asked Ally to watch over her grandmother. Tessa was a vibrant and sassy eighty-two-year-old who knew everything about everyone in town—much like the rest of the population of tiny Pepper, Mia included.

Well, *almost* everything—not even Lucy knew Ally's deepest, most revolting secret, and she planned to keep it that way. Which wouldn't be very difficult now that Lucy had decided to stay in Ashtown permanently. She planned to take Tessa back with her, too. Leaving the town—and Ally—in her dust.

"Oh, she's doing fine," she twisted her fingers in her long, brown waves as she fought yet another wave of anxiety. "I'll let you know when Lucy's coming back. Later!"

She barely gave Mia time to say a word before she spun and rushed out the door. She spent every waking minute trying to *not* think about Lucy—literally her only friend in the world—deserting her. Of course, that was impossible. She didn't resent Lucy finding the love of her life and everything that came with it, but... what about Ally?

Guilt assailed her, and she felt childish for even thinking such things, but sometimes it couldn't be helped. She'd spent so long on her own that when she'd run into Lucy years after high school ended, she'd held on for dear life. Now, Lucy and Tessa were the only family she'd been able to lay claim to for longer than she cared to remember.

Ducking down a side street, Ally headed for a familiar route home. The narrow path along the forest—made by deer, according to her wolf—bordered private property. It was gated off from the world, but the world didn't have a determined inner wolf who sniffed out an opening. Once she snuck in, the path was hidden from view by a latticework of white and yellow honeysuckles that twined along the chain link fence.

Breathing deep, a smile tugged at her lips as the air filled her. She could practically taste the sweetness of the honeysuckle. The sun's bright rays snuck past the rustling leaves, casting dappled shadows across the forest floor. A bird sang from the branches of a nearby tree and she was sure she heard a squirrel racing through the underbrush.

Pepper would be different without Lucy, but maybe she could continue to call this place home. Her wolf liked the quiet and lack of overwhelming scent of pollution. There were forests and trees and plenty of prey for her animal to hunt. Maybe… She closed her eyes and took another deep breath. She expected those same soothing scents to fill her lungs but… But she nearly choked as a new aroma filled her nose. One that sent a bolt of fear down her spine and caused her heartbeat to stutter.

It had to be the dogs, right? She'd been walking the pups and their scent was confusing her nose. Because what she thought she smelled she didn't *really* smell.

Denial isn't just a river in Egypt, Ally.

The scent held an essence of smoke, cherry wood, and warm fur.

She swallowed hard and fought to draw air into her lungs. Another wolf had walked this path. Recently.

An all-too-familiar urge to race home, grab her go-bag and get the hell out of Dodge rushed forward. It didn't matter that the scent wasn't *his*. The fact that a strange wolf prowled around teeny, tiny Pepper was bad enough. Because there was never only one. She'd learned from experience that where there was one, there were more.

She'd had a good run—more than a few months in one place had seemed almost decadent to her and she'd made it *years*. But it was her own damn fault for getting comfortable, for letting herself think she might actually be able to settle down in one spot forever, surrounded by people who cared about her.

She cared for them even more. Which meant it was time to go. Attachments weren't a good thing in life.

With wolves in the area, Tessa would be safer with her gone. Besides, the older woman would be moving to Ashtown with Lucy any day now. The timing couldn't have been better for Ally to hit the road. Just as she had a dozen times before.

She quickened her steps, managing to take a half-dozen strides before her wolf rushed forward. It fought for control, tugging at the reins and fighting her forward momentum. She struggled against the strength of her wolf, ignoring its snarls and growls as she tried to continue. Tried and failed. Even when she told it to quit being such a stubborn ass, it held on and refused to budge.

What the hell!

The beast surged then, attempting to force her shift, but she beat it back into submission… for now, anyway. That didn't mean it was done. The animal ached to chase this new, delicious smelling wolf. To capture more of its scent and wallow in its natural flavors.

No way. She mentally shook her head at the beast. Ally wouldn't risk it. If they'd learned anything from the past, it was that no good could come from being around their kind. Too much pain, too much torment. Had it already forgotten the harshest, most painful lesson?

The beast whined, wanting to comfort its terrified human

half but still controlled by its animal instincts. *Chase. Protect. Hunt. Calm. Stalk. Comfort.*

It retreated at the final thought—the wolf attempting to comfort its human half. It didn't withdraw fully, the beast still hovering just beneath her skin, but it was enough for Ally to resume control. When she came back to herself, she realized she'd bent over, one hand clinging to the chain link fence to keep her upright. Her skin shone with a sheen of perspiration, thoughts of the past forcing her long buried panic to rise.

She wasn't sure what was up with the wolf and had no idea why it was suddenly all keen on finding another of their kind. It could feel the agony from their shared memories, experiencing them just as keenly as her human half. So why was it so eager to chase trouble? Then again, she'd never understood much about her wolf all together. That was what came from being forced... She mentally shoved that thought aside and straightened fully.

"Thank you," she muttered and returned to her path.

She kept her nose attuned to every scent that drifted past her. Maybe the strange wolf was simply passing through Pepper on his way somewhere else. Maybe it wasn't time to panic...yet. If he stuck around, she could decide whether to hightail it out of town—or set her wolf on him.

Then again, what if he'd been hired to hunt her down?

Only one person on earth would do that—her ex-boyfriend, Brian Riverson. He'd vowed to stop at nothing to find her, dead or alive. A shudder wracked her frame, causing her to stumble to her knees. She stayed where she was, unhurt but panting as if she was experiencing tremendous pain.

It was the memory of pain, she knew that, but it felt as fresh as the day it happened. She could almost see the leering faces of the jackals Brian had called his pack mates. She could almost feel their claws dragging against her flesh. She could almost smell Brian's sour, cloying scent. It clung to her lungs, lingered in her nose. It reeked of rotten garbage and wet dog and spilled blood.

Ally lowered her head and struggled to calm her breathing. She was having a panic attack, nothing more. She could handle this. Internet research had taught her deep breathing techniques. On her first deep breath, the pain eased. On her second deep breath, the jackals in her mind faded. On the third deep breath… she still smelled him. She took another breath, then another. Still there. Still there and fresh and still as slick and disgusting as ever.

"Shit!"

It was *him*. He'd found her. The scent wasn't imaginary. It was real and based on the strength, he'd been past only minutes before. Nausea gripped her stomach and rose into her throat, but she fought it back. She pummeled it into submission. She needed her wits about her if *he* was on the prowl. No matter what happened, she wouldn't be taken out mid-vomit.

A nearby bird cawed, a loud call before it burst into the air, sending leaves raining down on her. She glanced around at her surroundings, searching for *him* among the trees. And that was when she realized exactly how stupid she was. She'd found the perfect path for him, hadn't she? She practically handed herself to him on a silver platter. The path was isolated, hidden from view, and had more than one blind corner.

He could be hiding around the next bend for all she knew. Him and one of his goons, just waiting to jump out at her. He'd brought that strange wolf—that other scent she couldn't identify—with him. Side by side, they'd come after her.

Her inner wolf tried to argue that the owner of the other scent wasn't necessarily working with *him*. Ally almost snorted aloud. Right. She didn't believe in coincidence.

Her heart thundered so loud she was sure it could be heard in outer space, the rumble constantly increasing in speed. She whirled in place and raced back the way she'd come. She broke into a sprint, pushing her body to hurry over the rotten leaves and dirt. For the first time in her adult life, Ally *wanted* to be surrounded by people, in full view of the world. Witnesses. She needed witnesses when *he* finally found her. Knowing him, he'd corner her somewhere. He'd want her afraid, trembling and filled with panic. Then he'd strike.

The last time she'd been in his presence, he'd turned her into a werewolf. That was when he'd wanted her as his "mate." That was when she'd escaped, and she'd turned him into a failure.

The Riverson family—Brian Riverson—didn't accept failure. This time, he'd kill her.

CHAPTER TWO

Kade stared at his cell phone, a mix of reluctance and loyalty to his brother warring inside him. On one hand, he didn't want to get bitched at. On the other, Mason wasn't *only* his older brother, but also his alpha. And when the Blackwood Alpha called, the wolf better pick up.

Dammit.

He tapped the green circle on the screen and placed the phone against his ear. "This is Kade."

Mason skipped pleasantries and his irritated voice blared through the phone's speaker. "So, how's Tessa? You remember Tessa, right? Eighty-two. An older version of my mate? Ring any bells?"

Kade knew his brother's question was rhetorical. If

Mason expected an answer, then Kade was a pretty princess in a pink tutu. At the moment he sported his typical snug shirt, worn jeans, and boots that'd seen better days. No tutu in sight.

"Now, Mason—" Kade tried to soothe the angry wolf, but his brother's growl interrupted him.

"Don't *even* try to tell me you haven't found her. Hell, you didn't even have to look. I gave you her address."

Kade scrubbed a hand over his stubbly jaw. "Yeah. I know, but—"

"But what? What can you possibly say to excuse the fact you've been gone for a week and haven't even knocked on the woman's door?"

Kade chewed on the inside of his cheek. He had something to show for his time in Pepper, Georgia. It just wasn't anything his brother would want to hear about. Such as how he'd spent the last week tracking down the sweet smell of a deliciously tempting female wolf. So far, the closest he'd come to finding the mystery wolf was a ponytail band she'd worn. Her sweet honey and milk scent still clung to it and he wore it on his wrist as a reminder of his personal mission.

He was going to find this woman.

He just had to get his brother off his back first.

"You seriously have nothing to say for yourself?" Mason demanded, dragging Kade back into the conversation. "I called Tessa, you know. She hasn't so much as had a phone call from you."

"Fine, fine," Kade grumbled, "I'll take care of it."

Being the brother of the pack's Alpha wasn't all fun and games. Just when he wanted to reach through the phone and punch Mason square in the jaw, he had to remind himself that his brother was the most dominant wolf in the pack—their leader. As the leader, he rightfully expected everyone—including his younger siblings—to fall in line. Normally, Kade was fine with going along with everything.

Unfortunately, this situation sure as hell wasn't normal.

"Whatever's going on—" Mason continued with authority, his brother's dominance vibrating through the phone and stirring his wolf. The beast tucked its tail between its legs, not liking that its alpha was angry. "—and for God's sake don't tell me what it is—you're going to complete the mission I assigned you. Get your ass to Tessa's. Do not pass go, do not collect two hundred dollars. Once inside, pack up that little old lady, along with all of her and Lucy's shit, and haul it all back to Ashtown. No questions. No hesitation. Is that understood?"

Kade grunted, his wolf's instincts fighting a vicious battle inside him. They should listen to their alpha, but that female... "I said I'd take care of it and I will." His beast howled its objection, desperate to find that little female. "Don't get your tail in a twist."

He wasn't sure if he was talking to his brother or his own inner animal.

"Seriously? You're going there?" The gravelly edge of Mason's voice annoyed him even more than the commanding tone. "Do you know what it's like to have a mate so desperate to get her things and her grandmother that she literally will not stop asking you about it? Every time I turn around, she's there asking if you're on your way. Then I get the joy of having to say, 'No, he's still in Pepper, doing God knows what.' Then she gives me sad eyes and this little pout, and her voice gets all soft. How do you think that makes me, *your alpha*, look in front of my new mate? I can't even get my brother to bring me one old lady."

Kade rubbed the back of his neck, wincing at the picture Mason painted. "Well—"

"Not to mention I nearly step on a damn cat every time I move. This place is crawling with kittens. It's a biblical plague, except we have tiny furballs instead of locusts." Mason huffed. "I think I'd prefer locusts."

"But I—"

"Whatever your excuse, Kade, I don't give a single, solitary rat's ass—or cat's ass. I'm not happy. When I'm not happy, people get hurt. Right now, you're on the very top of my pain inducing to-do list. Now, Tessa is waiting for you, and if you know what's good for you, you'll get to her house sooner rather than later. Get me?"

Kade's jaw clenched and he fought to find even one snippet of calm. "Yeah, message received."

"Good. 'Cause I won't have this conversation again."

Mason ended the call without bothering to say goodbye. Not that he was surprised. Kade glared at his phone for a minute before shoving it in his back pocket.

Yeah, he was pissed at getting his ass chewed out, but he couldn't deny he'd been shirking his duties a bit. But if Mason had just *listened* to him for five seconds, he would have understood. Mason had just discovered his fated mate, after all, and his brother had stopped at nothing to have her. Mason couldn't expect Kade to act any different, even if he was supposed to be helping an old woman pack up her belongings.

Kade needed to find this she-wolf soon or he'd go insane. For the last week, her scent had led him throughout town. Sometimes she'd crisscross her own trail, others he'd scent her along the very outskirts of the small town, and then he'd catch her flavors when strolling down Front Street. She liked to walk, that much was certain. The part that confused him, though, was that her scent was usually mingled with that of dogs. Werewolves enjoyed pet dogs about as much as they enjoyed pet cats.

Not at all.

As far as Kade was concerned, he deserved a damn commendation. Even in his desperation to find this woman he recognized as his mate, he'd managed to keep his wolf contained. He'd kept a low profile—as commanded—which wasn't easy in a town as small as Pepper.

But thanks to Mason's demands, time was running out and Kade had little choice now. He needed to do as his alpha commanded. That didn't mean he'd give up on finding his mate. He simply had to accomplish both *before* Mason drove down and took matters into his own hands.

Kade knew—without a doubt—where to find Tessa. As for that delicious she-wolf... Maybe it was time to "loosely interpret" Mason's rules. He'd told Kade to lay low and not draw attention to himself. Well, shifting into a wolf and pretending to be a dog wouldn't draw attention, right?

Besides, the beast that lived inside him had a far keener sense of smell than he did. As much as he'd tried to avoid it—and as much as he'd denied his wolf's pleas—Kade had no choice but to shift and track down his mate the old-fashioned way.

He hurried down a side street and ducked behind some

shrubbery at the edge of the woods. He shrugged out of his clothes and tucked them, along with his wallet and phone, deep under a bush. He could retrieve them when he was done with his hunt and returned. He didn't think walking around naked would be considered "low profile."

Kade loosened the ties on his wolf and the delighted beast bounded forward. He relaxed into the sensations of his shift, letting his animal take the lead while his body lengthened and expanded. The tingle of fur sprouting all over his body came with the prick of his fangs poking into the lips of his growing snout. The familiar thrill of a predator chasing its prey zipped through his bulky, wolf body.

Once on all fours, Kade took a deep breath, his damp nose held high in the air as he searched for the woman's scent. His upper lip peeled back, frustrated that he didn't smell her immediately. Darting out from the underbrush, he loped down the path edging the woods, sniffing and snuffling as he went. He'd already searched the area earlier, but he wanted to make sure he didn't miss anything. Having his wolf senses at his disposal meant he'd pick up everything now.

And he did.

Only a handful of feet down the trail, he caught a hint of that intoxicating aroma. Her sweet scent mingled with the honeysuckles growing on a nearby fence, and he couldn't help but yip with the rush of joy that hit him. *Damn*, she smelled good! So good he couldn't wait to strip her bare and coat himself in her scent. Then he'd claim her. Sink his cock and fangs into his mate and tie them together for eternity.

His.

Nose to the ground, he followed her trail, pausing when he reached a higher concentration of her scent. The smell lingered there, stronger than before but tinged with the overwhelming sting of fear. Not just fear. No, it was utter terror. A growl rumbled to life within his chest, his wolf hating that their mate feared anything—anyone.

Because as his beast grumbled and growled, he caught a whiff of another wolf in the area. A wolf that set the fur along his spine on end. A wolf his beast ached to kill even if he wasn't sure why. That growl grew, volume steadily increasing as he searched the surrounding area. He hunted this other shifter, determined to eliminate the cause of his mate's fear. If he remained near...

But no amount of searching brought him a fresher trail. That, coupled with the fact that the she-wolf's scent had stopped suddenly at this spot on the trail, meant she must have turned back.

Kade backtracked until he picked up her fresher flavors. *Very* fresh. So fresh he couldn't help but lick his whiskers and drool just a little. He could practically taste her on his tongue, the heady combination of sugar and female. He followed it, attention solely on the trail. The one that led toward the middle of town.

Yeah, a panting, drooling wolf running around the streets of tiny Pepper might be a cause for alarm. He stayed in the shadows, hoping residents would think he was simply a big, dumb, happy dog instead of the dangerous beast that lived inside him.

His claws clicked on the sidewalk as he scanned the street for her. Her smell filled his nose, so he knew she was close, but didn't even catch one flicker of her presence. He stopped just before his street intersected with Front Street and Kade carefully poked his head around the corner building. If he was going to get spotted by some random local, it would be on the main street running through town.

He scanned up one side and down the other and before his eyes landed on any other Pepper resident, he found her. His gaze was drawn to her full hips, the way they swayed as she hurried across the street. Her dark brown hair fell in soft waves down her back and undulated as she walked. So did all the best parts of her curvy body. He'd won the jackpot! No, he'd won every jackpot across the globe all at once.

He couldn't wait to learn her name, to hold her hand, to kiss those soft, pink lips, to know every last thing about her. But first he had to catch up to her.

Now! his wolf insisted.

As she reached the opposite sidewalk, Kade bounded out from behind the building. His claws scraped against the concrete sidewalk, nails searching for purchase as he leapt off the curb and... into the path of an oncoming car.

CHAPTER THREE

Ally's heart thundered, pounding so loud she wasn't sure any other sound could penetrate the steady rhythm.

She just wanted to go home. No stops along the way. No check-ins or "how are yas." Not that home would be safe from Brian. A wooden door wouldn't be much of a deterrent, but there was something to be said for being familiar with the lay of the land. At the very least, she knew where to find the knife block.

She kept her eyes trained on the front door of the house she shared with Tessa as she strode up the walkway. Relative safety was so close. Fifteen feet. Then twelve. Then…

The high-pitched shriek of tires skidding across asphalt. The ear-piercing yelp of an animal. Ally whirled in place, instincts sending her spinning to face the road just in time to watch a large furry body flip end over end through the air. A red sedan with tinted windows sat motionless in the middle of the street but by the time the big dog thudded to the ground, it was gone in another waft of smoking rubber.

"Asshole!" she snarled at the motorist as she rushed to the near motionless dog. The only sign it still lived was the rise and fall of its chest.

The car neared the corner and whipped onto a side street and... did she catch a hint of Brian's noxious scent? Instincts battled one another, her fear urging her to run to the house while another part of her demanded she stay put.

What the? That was when she caught it—a scent that her wolf recognized before Ally's human mind could process the discovery. The dog bleeding at her feet wasn't a dog. No, it was a wolf—a werewolf just like her.

Like Brian.

And it wasn't just any werewolf. It was the wolf she'd smelled on the edge of the woods. His familiar smoky scent set her wolf to howling. It demanded to be released, but Ally shushed the thing and knelt next to the furry body.

The wolf's chest moved steadily, and it appeared to have suffered only scrapes. On the side of the road, there was no way to tell if it had broken bones or internal bleeding.

The very thought tightened her chest, as if he meant more to her than just another wolf she'd stumbled across. Her wolf snarled at her, doing its best to tell her that this wolf was a hell of a lot more than some random shifter.

She nearly snorted. Yeah, right. They didn't know the werewolf from Adam. He could be just as dangerous as her ex, or even more so. She would be safer far from him.

Even if he made her skin all tingly and sent her heart to racing for a reason that had nothing to do with fear or panic. It had everything to do with watching him shift, touching his skin, exploring every inch—

Right. Not going there.

A quick glance in both directions confirmed she and the mangy mutt weren't about to become roadkill, but another car would come along soon enough. Muttering an oath under her breath, she reached a shaking hand out and stroked its thick coat. Her eyes fell closed and her breath quickened at the softness of his fur. Her wolf surged again, fighting her for control, but she held it at bay.

Ally had spent her adult life learning how to fight off her inner beast. Yet, even with those countless hours fighting an internal battle with the wolf, it nearly won this round. It *really* wanted to get its paws on this wolf.

She reached for the downed wolf, and at her touch, he stirred. A soft whine rose from his chest and he opened his eyes, his soft brown gaze latching onto hers. Warmth flooded her, the comfort of his presence nearly overwhelming her decision to keep her distance. Indecision warred with her wolf's certainty. It drove her to care for him—protect him. After years of its encouragement to stay away from other wolves, it now wanted her to get close to *this* male. That sudden flip was enough to spur her into movement. Enough to break the spell his nearness wove around her.

She glanced up and down the street once more, still not finding any cars that threatened their safety.

The wolf twisted and rolled until his feet settled beneath his body, but the very moment he attempted to stand, he flopped back to its side. A low whimper reached her ears and those big brown eyes met hers for a moment, before his head dropped to the road once more.

The dog lover part of her couldn't stand seeing an animal —werewolf or otherwise—in pain, but her survival instincts warned her to steer clear of any and all werewolves. Personal experience had taught her wolves healed quickly from all types of vile abuse. A lesson taught to her by Brian himself.

This one wasn't so far gone he wouldn't heal, of that much she was sure, but it would take a little while. He wouldn't be lumbering off to lick his wounds any time soon. Which left her with a choice: leave him in the road to risk getting hit by another car or drag his furry ass into her house and risk being eaten by a sadistic psychopath.

"Shit," she muttered again. "Shit, shit, shit."

Kneeling, she wrapped her arms under his forelegs and hauled him upright. The length of his body pressed against hers, his scent and nearness sending her wolf into a ravenous frenzy. It took everything she had to half-carry the beast without letting her own gain control.

"You're one lucky pup," she growled into his ear, grunting while she hefted him to the front door. "Not even The Rock would be able to haul your heavy ass this far."

A sound rumbled from the wolf, but she ignored him.

"What the hell were you thinking, anyway? Shifting in the middle of a human town in broad daylight." She clicked her tongue. "You must be out of your damn mind. You're lucky you *only* got hit by a car. Some of the hunters around here would be thrilled to hang a wolf's head on their wall."

Ally fumbled with her keys and the doorknob, finally releasing the latch so she could bump the door open with her hip. She paused and listened, her wolf enhancing her senses for a moment. She thanked God that Tessa was so predictable. Like she did every day, she was at her morning "stitch 'n' bitch" with the head librarian. Which meant Ally had about an hour to figure out what the hell she was going to do with *him*.

With a grunt, she heaved the wolf inside and kicked the door shut with her heel.

"You may be nuts, but I'm fucking insane for helping you." She glared at the wolf in her arms. "Now, if you even *look* at Tessa the wrong way, I will go feral she-wolf all over your mangy ass."

Hopefully the guy's super wolfy healing powers would allow her to kick him out long before Tessa returned, but knowing her luck, that wouldn't be the case. If he'd only suffered scrapes and a concussion, he would have been on four paws already. She paused in the entryway, mind whirling as she tried to think of a place to deposit Mr. McWooferton while he finished his healing. Somewhere Tessa wouldn't go snooping around while he got better. Somewhere Ally wouldn't be cooped up with an injured wolf while he healed.

Neither of those was Ally's room, but there *was* a room not being occupied at the moment. Plus, it'd been mostly packed already. Lucy wouldn't mind, right? She nibbled her lower lip, stuck in a whirl of indecision. It was the wolf that made the choice for her. He whined and shifted in her hold, spurring her onward—to Lucy's old room.

It took five minutes of huffing, puffing and cursing before she managed to reach Lucy's room and heave him onto the handmade quilt covering the bed. She made a silent apology to her BFF along with a pinky swear to have the quilt dry cleaned once she got rid of the furball. Her main saving grace was that at least his scrapes had stopped bleeding.

At least until she took a look at them and dug out whatever had embedded itself in his wounds.

She propped her hands on her hips and stared down at the pathetic wolf. "If I'm doing this, I'm doing it right, puppy." She huffed. "Don't say I didn't warn ya."

She left him for a moment, striding through the house to fetch the first aid kit and other supplies, before returning to his side. He hadn't budged while she'd been gone, those dark eyes still closed and chest hardly moving.

Dropped to her knees beside the bed, she dug through the kit and snagged what she needed. Then she went to work. Fingers sifted through dense fur, carefully wiping at the matted blood to get to the injury beneath. She prodded each pink patch of skin, feeling for any abnormality hidden from view.

Each time she located an odd lump beneath his flesh, she pulled out her razor blade and went to work. A slice. An extraction. Then a dab of disinfectant. And every one of her cuts drew a low, whining moan from the wolf. His body tensed, and lips curled back to reveal his fangs, but he remained in place. He fought his instincts for her, battling to remain passive when his animal probably wanted to tear her to shreds for causing him pain.

Damn, he was strong as hell.

"I'm almost done." She murmured and moved on from his flank, gentle as she addressed each scrape and gash. Then she was even more careful when she got to his chest.

A deep gash bisected his chest, and she knew she'd been wrong about the whole "he's done bleeding" thing. Red liquid still seeped from the long cut and a closer look revealed a smattering of white visible beneath the thick fluid. This one had gone all the way to the bone. She cringed, hurting on his behalf. She'd healed from an injury like that in the past and it'd been utter hell.

Instead of poking, prodding, and patting the wound, she grabbed the half-empty bottle of hydrogen peroxide. She twisted off the cap and set it aside before holding the brown bottle over his body. Biting her lip, she tipped the container until the clear liquid flowed from the top, pouring the bubbling fluid into his wound. Bubbles immediately filled the channel of the gash, blocking out the red of his blood.

That was when the wolf lost control. His eyes sprung open and his jaws parted while a snarl leapt from his chest. Utter fury edged with pain radiated from his feral expression and she forced herself to remain still. She couldn't run, no matter how much her body decided that sprinting in the opposite direction was a good idea.

Wolves liked the chase.

That rumbling continued, not faltering a bit as the fur

surrounding his wound retreated into his flesh. The wolf's fur moved in a rippling wave as the beast withdrew and allowed his human half to emerge. Bones snapped, and muscles stretched and reformed as more of his inner animal withdrew until she soon had a naked man spread before her.

And she was perverted enough to look her fill. Because holy hotness…

He was massive. His size had him taking up most of the bed and the strength of his wolf was echoed in the man's heavily muscled body. Each one looked as if it was carved from granite, the harsh lines practically begging for her touch.

There was another part of him she'd like to touch—explore—but she avoided staring at his dangly bits. She wasn't a creeper. Even if creeping on him was very, very tempting. *No. Bad Ally.*

Her visual travels moved on and their eyes clashed for a split second, brown eyes flashing amber before pain dragged him into unconsciousness once more. His dark eyebrows furrowed in his unconscious state. Either he was dreaming or in pain, and judging by the wound on his chest, it was the latter.

The fine stubble peppering his jaw hinted that he'd been too busy to shave for at least a few days. The planes and angles under the whiskers looked like cut glass, contrasting his soft, supple lips. Lips her wolf urged her to kiss.

Hell, her beast urged her to do more than swap spit with the wolf. Visions of stripping before crawling into bed next to him ran through her head on a loop. She'd bury her fingers in his dark chocolate colored hair and then let her hands roam his thick, hard body. Would he be hard all over? Even *there?*

Nope, not going there. I'm just not.

There would be no naked explorations. Long ago she'd learned that some of the ugliest things in the world could come in the prettiest packages.

And this guy was too damn pretty.

CHAPTER FOUR

Kade drew in a long, deep breath, searching his surroundings by scent instead of sight. The world tilted and spun around him, warning him to keep his eyes closed. The soft surface beneath him coupled with the cool temperature indicated he was inside…. Somewhere. But where? He searched through his memories, trying to figure out what the hell had happened. All he managed to accomplish was causing his head to pound and spin once again while his stomach threatened to crawl up his throat.

Awesome.

Kade's wolf did not appreciate his sarcasm.

He took another deep breath and this time his senses brought him good news. His mate's scent filled his lungs. His milk and honey mate had been near. That knowledge stabilized him, gave him something other than nausea to focus on. Wherever he'd landed, she'd been there, and recently. Which meant she had to have sensed what he already knew—they were mates.

He released his breath in a slow exhale and forced his eyes to open. It took a moment for his eyes to focus, but soon a white popcorn-textured ceiling came into view. He tilted his head as much as he dared and scanned his surroundings. An old rocker and grandfather clock sat in the corner. Against the wall was an antique dresser. A thin quilt covered his naked body, and he moved his head slightly to find that his head nestled in goose down pillows.

A bedroom, then. He had no memory of how he'd arrived, but he was in someone's bedroom. Concentrating as hard as he could, he forced his mind to recall what had brought him to this bed. He'd been in wolf form and spotted his mate crossing the street. He'd run after her, and then... Nothing.

The screech of tires reached through the window, the sound bringing the rest of his memories to the forefront. His impulsive wolf had been so focused on its mate, it had acted like a pup and run into the street without looking both ways. The sensation of hard steel colliding with his ribs, then flipping through the air, and finally landing with a painful thud. Then everything went black.

His mate must have seen the accident and brought him into her home. He spotted a bottle of hydrogen peroxide, some bloodied cotton balls and a tube of antibiotic cream on the bedside table and their presence made his heart warm.

That sensation of warmth was put on hold when he was interrupted by tinkling laughter from somewhere below him.

My mate! His wolf joined him and released a yip followed by a happy howl.

Kade placed a palm on the soft mattress and pushed against the soft surface. He tensed his abs and struggled to sit up. He couldn't remain in bed when his mate was so near.

Pain put a stop to his attempt, though. A hot ice pick of pain shot through his chest and every muscle screamed its objection to movement. Yeah, well, it was happening. He gripped the bed post and used it to hold himself steady as he pushed to his feet. He shuffled across the room, the lingering aches making walking difficult, but he was determined to reach the full-length mirror near the door.

He paused when his reflection came into view and he scanned his body. A bright red scar cut across his chest, obviously the largest of his wounds. It had already closed, and would no doubt be fully healed by night fall. The bruises along his ribs had already yellowed and the handful of scrapes he'd suffered were all but gone.

He'd be good as new by morning. Unfortunately, today he'd suffer from his wolf's recklessness.

Asshole.

Instead of experiencing even an ounce of guilt, the beast paced inside him, demanding they follow their mate's scent until they tracked her down and claimed her forever. Kade thought it might be a good idea to learn her name first. The wolf snorted at him.

Of course, the odds of successfully finding and claiming her would be greatly improved if he wasn't buck naked and two seconds from falling over. He carefully made his way to the closet and dug around in search of something to wear. Except he came up empty. For clothes, anyway. He *did* find two dozen jigsaw puzzles and fifty back issues of *Redbook*.

"Crap," he grumbled.

The dresser didn't yield anything more useful. Nothing but drawer after drawer of moth-eaten, gaudy afghans in a variety of bizarre patterns. God, there wasn't even an old chenille robe! He tugged out a neon pink blanket edged in bright purple and wrapped it around his hips. Desperate times called for desperate measures and Kade—and his wolf—were desperate to be near their mate.

Kade eased the bedroom door open and stepped into a wide hallway. He used his nose to follow the sweet scent of his mate and he couldn't help but smile at the sound of her laughter once again. He carefully traveled down the old, worn stairs, unable to stop himself from scanning the pictures lining the wall. Each one showed the same girl throughout the years. From her time as a cute baby held by an older woman until she grew into a gawky preteen with a softball bat slung over one shoulder. Then she was a beautiful young woman in a college cap and gown, one arm draped around the shoulders of a stout, older woman.

That last photo drew him up short. Those blue eyes, blonde hair, and familiar face had him freezing in place. The girl in the photos was Lucy, his brother's newfound mate. Which meant the older woman had to be Lucy's grandmother—

"Tessa!" The young woman's voice was a mixture of scandalized and suppressed laughter.

"What?" came a hoarse response. "I can't believe you didn't sneak a peek. Didn't anyone teach you how to play nurse?"

Kade blinked. And then blinked again, following it up with a shake of his head. Somehow, he'd wound up where he was supposed to be without even *trying*.

He reached the bottom of the steps and turned left, following those voices until he finally stepped into the archway of a kitchen. His mate's scent overwhelmed him then, sinking into his pores and overwhelming his other senses. Nothing existed beyond him and his mate. He scanned the small space, his gaze immediately going to her. He'd only caught a glimpse of her beauty earlier and now that they were face-to-face... She stole his breath away.

One look and words were erased from his memory, her mere appearance enough to make him mute. He vibrated with need for her, and he struggled against his wolf's desire to stalk her, hold her, and claim her right there on the kitchen floor. And counter. And table. Then back to the floor, maybe.

Against the refrigerator?

His body responded to his fantasy, cock twitching and pressing against the obnoxious afghan around his waist. Being so close to her, so near her heat and the purity of her scent, he struggled to keep his wolf—and body —contained.

Baseball. Old people getting it on. Falling off a cliff. Damn, no matter what he thought of, his body refused to calm.

Kade gritted his teeth and forced himself to focus on the world around him and *not* on the glorious woman mere feet away. He pushed the wolf back and slammed it into its mental cage, which gave him a little relief from the constant drive to take her. But there was still part of him...

Yeah, he needed to get control of his horny ass.

He shook his head and truly focused on his mate, meeting her stare. Her *hostile* stare. Her eyes were narrowed in a tight glare and her body remained tense. As if she was ready to pounce and destroy him, but... why? He didn't *think* he'd done anything anger-worthy after the crash. He hadn't been awake long, but he couldn't have offended her while unconscious, right? His wolf snorted, the beast trying to remind him of that one time in second grade when—

Kade cut the animal off at its knees and wrapped a thick as hell blanket around the mental cage as well. He didn't want any comments from the peanut gallery.

His mate stared at him and he stared at her staring at him and... And after what felt like an eternity, the old woman stepped forward. She grinned up at him, meeting his eyes for a moment before her stare traveled the length of his body. Her gaze slid all the way down to his toes and then up once more before giving him an even wider smile.

"Well, *hello there.*" The woman cocked her head to get a better view of that area below the waist.

Kade cleared his throat and raised an eyebrow. He put his hand in front of his cock and snapped his fingers. "My eyes aren't down there."

Tessa laughed, the wide smile making the years melt away, and she extended her hand. "Sorry, it's not every day a handsome, almost-naked man ends up in my kitchen. I'm Tessa Morgan and this is my friend Ally Rose."

Ally Rose. He let her name roll around in his mind for a moment, allowing it to sink into him. His mate had a name—one that perfectly suited her—Ally Rose.

"Kade," he replied with a smile. He gently took Tessa's birdlike hand in his own. "And I think you've been expecting me. Lucy sent me to help you move to Ashtown."

Ally's eyebrows shot up, but Tessa slapped her thigh and barked out a throaty laugh. "It's a pleasure to meet you, Kade," Tessa said, tipping him a playful wink before growing serious. "Ally told me about your accident. She saw the whole thing. I can't believe someone would just leave you in the street like that."

As far as he knew, Tessa was ignorant of the shifter world, which meant Ally had probably left out the part about him being a wolf when he was hit. He didn't want to blow Ally's cover, but the last thing they needed was for Tessa to call the cops and report a hit and run.

"They were probably just scared. Besides, I barely got scratched. See?"

Ally's lips pressed together to form a thin line as Tessa stepped closer to inspect his body. All that remained were a few red marks and some old-looking bruises. Tessa shifted slightly, and if he hadn't known any better he would have sworn the old woman was trying to see between the holes of the blanket. The woman was over eighty. She wouldn't be trying to… Then again, Lucy had said her grandmother was "frisky."

"Still…" Her eyes lingered on the quickly deflating mound at his groin for a moment, before she met his gaze. "What happened to your clothes?"

Right. What happened to his clothes? "I, uh—"

"I threw them out," Ally cut him off. "They, um… They were a mess, so I got rid of them."

Tessa's grey eyes sparkled with mischief. "I should have known. How many times do I have to tell you to be more careful when ripping off men's clothes? The poor boys need something to wear home, dear."

Men?

His eyes snapped to Ally, and jealousy consumed his entire being. A low growl rumbled deep in his throat before he could suppress the sound. It was too low for Tessa's human hearing, but Ally's wolf didn't have that problem. It also didn't like him growling. Her eyes widened with fear for a split second and then that emotion was replaced with anger. She carefully grasped Tessa's frail wrist and pulled the older woman away from him.

Did she think he'd hurt a little old lady? *Shit.*

Damn, she was one wary wolf. She went to suspecting the worst before even giving him a chance to explain himself. She heard a growl and immediately jumped to the conclusion that he meant Tessa harm. That was the last thing he'd do and not only because Tessa was his Alpha Bitch's grandmother. Tessa was a female, old, and human —three very good reasons to keep his paws to himself.

But why did she expect the worst without them exchanging a word? He mentally shook his head and commiserated with his whining beast. It hated her mistrust and the heavy weight of anger pointed at him. Unfortunately, it wasn't something that could be fixed with the snap of a finger. It'd require gaining her trust slowly, carefully. But how?

He wracked his brain while Ally helped Tessa take her seat at the kitchen table. Maybe if he got his mate alone...

"I've got more clothes at my motel, but I'm not sure how Pepper feels about public nudity."

Tessa lit up like a Fourth of July fireworks display. "Ally will drive you wherever you need to go."

Ally looked as though someone had slapped her, but her lips remained pressed together in that harsh line.

"You never get out of the house." Tessa patted Ally's hand and then gave her a little nudge. "Take your time and get some fresh air while you drive Kade to the motel."

Ally glared. Kade smiled. And Tessa cackled with glee.

Hell, he almost joined her with the cackling. Sitting alone in a car with Ally—no distractions, no interruptions, no little old lady eyeballing his junk?

That sounded like heaven.

CHAPTER FIVE

Sitting alone in a car with Kade? Yeah, that sounded like Ally's version of hell.

Kade's gaze caressed her and Tessa simply grinned, tipping her head toward the door as if to move them along. Saying no wasn't a viable option, not after everything Tessa and Lucy had done for her. They'd given her a place to live when she'd had nothing and no one. Now, they were the only family she had.

Her love for them was greater than her wariness of this strange wolf. A wolf who somehow knew Lucy. What had her friend gotten herself into *now*?

It didn't matter. She'd figure it out. Just as soon as she got away from Kade, so she could think straight. Because at the moment, her wolf wanted to bare her belly for a nice rub from the hottie.

"Better get moving," Tessa apparently got tired of waiting on them to move and herded them toward the door that led to the garage. "Lucy's been waiting and there's no time to waste now. If I know my granddaughter, she's more than a little impatient."

Ally nodded and steeled her spine, preparing herself for what was to come—being locked up in a vehicle with Kade and surrounded by his scent.

She grabbed her small leather purse on her way out, not bothering to check if Kade followed. Of course, she didn't need to look for him. His scent wrapped around her like a cozy, warm blanket—growing stronger as she stepped into the garage.

She clenched her jaw and swallowed hard, doing her best to ignore the sensual molten heat flowing through her veins. To ignore the way her core throbbed at Kade's nearness. Her wolf howled for her to follow her body's lead, turn around and slam him against the wall. A quick rip would have the afghan in shreds and then she could truly jump his bones.

Not happening. She ignored the wolf's pleas and hopped into her silver Ford Focus. She loved her little car, the color and model chosen carefully. It was one of the most popular models from 2005 and silver had been the go-to color that year. Which meant there were a bajillion silver Focuses on the road and hers looked just like everyone else's. Bland. Generic. Forgettable. And hopefully, difficult for Brian to find.

"You don't drive the Granny Mobile?" he chuckled and flashed her a smile—was that a dimple?—while he nodded at the ancient Le Baron sitting next to her Focus.

Okay, first, dimples on a sexy guy needed to be against the law. It just wasn't fair. Second, the same needed to be applied to laughter that she felt to her toes and everywhere in between. Third, he was trying to charm her, and she *was not* going to be charmed by this hunk of hot fur.

Ally was surrounded by a ten-foot wall of steel and concrete. She was a cold, hard glacier with a heart to match. She was impervious to any emotions.

The garage door trundled open while he tugged open the car door. He lowered himself into the passenger seat, the afghan slipping open to reveal his bulging thigh.

And Ally wasn't looking or anything. She definitely wasn't wondering what else remained covered by the blanket. Nope, her eyes remained locked on the rearview mirror, stuck like glue, while her mind stayed focused on her task —getting the wolf's clothes.

"My stuff isn't far from here," he said as she backed out into the street. "After I get decent, we can grab my suitcase from the motel."

There was only one motel in Pepper, the Sleep Inn on the

other side of town. That meant even more time with him in an enclosed space. Ally held her breath for as long as she could while his scent filled the car, but as her vision dimmed, she allowed herself to breathe again. Passing out behind the wheel didn't seem like a good idea. Instead, she rolled the window down and sucked in the crisp outside air.

"Down the street and around the corner," he instructed quietly.

They fell into a tense silence, but it wasn't long before Kade shattered the quiet. "Can I ask you something?"

Ally hummed in response, careful to keep her attention on the road and not on the muscles of the half-naked man beside her.

"Why does your car smell like dog?" He sniffed. "Or rather, *dogs*."

"I'm a dog walker "

"Ah. Passion for animals?"

Ally shrugged. "As much as anyone else, I suppose."

Kade was shrewd and caught her ambivalence about her occupation. Sure, she loved animals, but getting dragged around by unruly mutts had never been her lifelong dream.

"Why do you do it then?"

"It's fun and easy and I can bug out in a hurry, if need be."

She tightened her grip on the wheel, knuckles turning white. She hadn't intended on sharing anything, much less something so revealing, to him. In fact, she'd tried very hard not to say anything at all. It just popped out. And it was something she'd never revealed to another soul. Ever.

His damn scent must have done something to her.

"Mind if I roll down your window?" Without waiting for an answer, she pressed the button to lower the glass and breathed in the fresh air until she almost couldn't smell his musk at all.

Almost.

"Why would you need to bug out?"

Dammit! Of course, he'd picked up on that. His curious gaze heated her cheeks until they burned. She cursed herself for opening her big mouth. Time for a change of subject.

"Why don't we focus on something else? Like, why the hell did Lucy send a werewolf to retrieve Tessa? Does she know what you really are?"

She hadn't meant to let herself slip into a sneer, but that was how it came out. Kade pretended not to notice, but she caught the way he tensed at her tone.

"Turn here. And yes, Lucy knows what I am."

Ally slowed to a stop at the cross street, thank God, because his next words might have sent the car careening into the corner market rather than onto the other road.

"I'm the Beta of the Blackwood pack just outside of Ashtown. My brother is the Alpha and Lucy is his mate."

Alpha.

Mate.

Alpha.

And Lucy was his *mate*.

Pain stabbed her in the gut and she curled over the steering wheel. The past surged, visions of teeth, flesh and blood consuming her thoughts. Her entire world centered around the violent images in her mind. Ally remembered all too well what happened when an Alpha decided he wanted a specific female for his mate. Shock and horror rolled over her, nearly stealing her sanity as the truth settled inside her.

Lucy was a werewolf. Like her.

Doomed to a life of misery. Like her.

Cursed. Like her.

Her heart shattered. Lucy was the kindest, sweetest person in the world. She'd suffered so much in her life and deserved better than a life tied to an Alpha. Horror was soon overcome by a tsunami of guilt and she wondered if she'd somehow been the cause behind Lucy's claiming.

"H-how?" She managed to push the words out of her mouth as she pulled into the intersection. She needed to distract herself by focusing on driving. Otherwise she'd shatter. She tapped the gas only to hear a blaring horn. A quick look revealed an oncoming car and she slammed her foot on the brake, bringing them to a jolting stop. All the while Kade stayed silent. The next time she was more careful and checked traffic before moving once again.

Once they were rolling along, Kade spoke again. "It was an accident. She jumped out in front of a car to save a pup's life."

That didn't surprise her. Lucy always gave everything to others even if she never received anything in return.

"The pup got scared and bit her. Thankfully, my brother found her before things got bad. They're very happy together."

Ally snorted her disbelief and rolled her eyes. And Ally was the Easter Bunny.

"*Right.*"

The weight of Kade's frown rested on her shoulders for a moment before he returned his gaze to the road. "Just up here on the right."

He pointed at a spot at the end of the street. Just beyond

the asphalt lay the path near the woods—where she'd first caught his scent.

And Brian's.

A tremble ran through her and she gritted her teeth, refusing to show weakness to the wolf at her side. He couldn't know how much he—and the news about Lucy—frightened her. It added another emotion to the mix, too.

Fury. At herself. At Lucy's "mate."

Why the hell hadn't Lucy called her? Ally would do anything for her!

Though the better question was why would Lucy have contacted her about anything wolf-y? Ally had never revealed her darkest secret. Had never explained what sent Ally careening into Pepper, intent on hiding from everyone and everything.

"Does Tessa know?" she asked.

Kade shook his head. "No. Their plan is to reveal it to her gently once she's settled in the pack house. They couldn't keep it a secret even if they wanted to and Lucy *definitely* doesn't want to."

That sounded like Lucy, which gave Ally a glimmer of hope that her friend wasn't living a life of utter despair and misery.

Kade reached for the door handle as he spoke. "How long

will it take you to pack up your things? Tessa wasn't kidding about Lucy getting impatient. I got my ass handed to me over the matter this morning by my brother, who apparently got his ass handed to him by Lucy."

When she didn't move, he settled back into his seat. She couldn't have heard him right. Her things? No, he had to be talking about Tessa.

"My things? Huh?"

"I can't imagine it will take long, since you're ready to 'bug out' at a moment's notice." His lips twitched a little and she curled her lip, glaring at him for laughing at her.

"Uh, why would I go anywhere?"

Sure, she wanted to see Lucy with her own eyes, but she wasn't sure she could force herself to walk into the territory of a pack of werewolves. The mere idea gave her a tight, bubbly feeling inside her chest. The firm grip of fear snared her, squeezing her in a strangling hold. It'd been a long time since her last panic attack, but this one promised to be a doozy. *Shit.*

Kade gave her a soft smile and rested his hand on hers, his fingers curling around her own where she still gripped the steering wheel. "We're mates, Ally. Can't you feel it?"

Something wrapped around her chest, compressing her ribs and snatching the ability to breathe out of reach. The pressure increased, tightening more and more the harder she fought for air. Her heart raced, threatening to burst from her chest, and she couldn't suppress the whimper as it vibrated in her throat.

Long ago, a different wolf had said those same words and she was *still* on the run from him.

What had she done in a past life to deserve *two* rabid psycho stalkers?

Except, was that an accurate description for Kade? When she was human, she hadn't been able to sense Brian's insanity. It was no wonder he'd been able to trick her. Now, her wolf's senses were sharper than ever, and she wasn't getting a "rabid stalker" vibe from Kade. He seemed so sincere, so gentle, despite his bulging muscles, which she was sure could do a lot of damage.

Fool me once... her brain whispered, and her wolf grumbled at her. It tried to tell her that she was wrong. Wrong about Lucy and wrong about Kade.

Yeah, Ally wasn't going there. She cleared her throat before speaking again. "If you keep to the shadows for a few feet, I think you can sneak into the woods without anyone seeing you."

"Sounds good." Kade nodded and slipped from the passenger seat before darting into the woods, the bright afghan trailing behind him.

And like the good little babysitter, Ally followed. Though

she moved like her blood had been replaced by molasses. She had to go with him on the off chance he was spied by one of Pepper's residents. At least with her at his side, she could sweet talk whoever saw the half-naked man traipsing through the woods.

If he were alone, he would have ended up face down and eating dirt courtesy of a half-dozen good old boys from the sheriff's office.

So, yeah, no matter how much she wanted to stay put and think about how a five-minute conversation changed her whole life, she slowly followed in Kade's wake.

Attention split between the hot werewolf and the forest floor, Ally allowed her whirling thoughts free reign.

Her best friend was a werewolf.

Her best friend would finally find out *she* was a werewolf.

And worst of all, another presumptuous, jerk male werewolf set his sights on her.

Her fingers twitched, and muscles tensed, human form anxious to leap back into her car and head for the hills. But she couldn't leave Tessa at the mercy of this strange werewolf. One who made her feel all sorts of funny things and drove her inner beast wild with his scent alone. He *seemed* nice enough, but she knew better than to trust him.

Wolves could never be trusted. Period.

In fact, he'd been out of her sight for far too long. She'd watched him duck out of sight behind a large gathering of bushes, but that'd been a bit ago. God only knew what he was up to now that she wasn't riding his ass.

Swallowing hard, she picked up her pace and followed Kade's scent. At least, until it was drowned out by a much stronger smell—one of rotten oranges and sickly wood.

Brian's scent. He'd been through here. Recently.

A twig snapped behind her and to the left. Ally spun, arms immediately raised and hands curled into fists. Adrenaline poured through her, body preparing to fight the owner of that scent. She'd lost a lot to Brian. She wasn't losing anything else.

Except it wasn't Brian at her back, but Kade.

She'd expected him to be less appealing once he covered himself. Unfortunately, she'd been wrong. With his muscles hidden from sight, she was tempted by him even more.

"Are you okay?" Concern flooded his expression. He took a step closer, brow furrowed. "I didn't mean to startle you."

She forced a small smile to her lips and pretended she was okay, even if her heart threatened to burst through her chest. With the imagined threat gone, her hands trembled, and she tucked them into her pockets. "I'm fine. Got everything?"

"Uh-huh." He nodded, and the look he shot her said he didn't believe a word she'd said.

Well, she *was* lying, so she couldn't blame him. He turned back the way they'd come and took a few steps before he stopped once more.

He cocked his head to the side and tipped it back, drawing in the air. He held the breath for a moment before lowering his attention to her. "Who's the other wolf?" A soft rumble peppered his words and Ally forced herself not to react to an angry wolf. "His scent is all over town. I don't like it."

Ally shrugged and strode past him toward the car. Desperation drove her. Desperation to get out of town and as far away from Brian Riverson as possible.

The sharp ring of a phone followed her and Kade sighed. "Shit. My cell phone. Hang on a sec."

Kade moved back through the undergrowth and Ally closed her eyes and focused on blocking the noxious odor. And failed miserably. The scent was simply too strong. Too fresh for her wolf to ignore. She needed to physically leave the area to be free of the stench. No amount of mind tricks, hoping, or praying would banish the smell.

A smell that got stronger as she stood there. It didn't

lessen with the breeze as it should. The wind should have snatched the flavors and spirited them away by now. Yet it hadn't. Opening her eyes again, she scanned the trees. Was he still close? Did he hide in the forest surrounding them?

And then she saw *it*. Something that had her gasping, heartbeat stuttering. A few feet away, letters carved deeply into the bark, an old tree had been vandalized. Its surface now marred with four letters.

A-L-L-Y.

Any delusional thoughts that she'd evaded Brian were destroyed in that moment. She'd played "pretend" and refused to accept that he was truly in the tiny town of Pepper, Georgia, but there was no denying the truth now.

There was another truth, as well. She needed to get away from Pepper as soon as possible. Now if she could have swung it, but that wasn't going to happen. Kade had spouted all this mate stuff. She didn't think he'd be okay with her disappearing into the wilds.

New plan. Tessa was almost packed, and it wouldn't take Ally long to tuck away what few things she'd acquired over the years. She could go with Kade and hope he could protect her from Brian's wrath.

Then, once they got to Ashtown, Ally could escape.

She was just... so tired. Tired of running. Tired of the constant fear. Tired of not having a life. Exhaustion led to mistakes, and if she made one false move, Brian would get her. She'd been lucky as hell to dodge him this long. It was only a matter of time before what little luck she had left vanished into thin air.

Except, unlike all the previous times she'd bolted, she had a place to go—even if it was temporary. Going to the wolf pack would be a risk, but the *possibility* of pain and death was a helluva lot better than the *certainty* she'd have with Brian.

Kade reappeared through the trees, more twigs snapping under his heavy gait as he moved, and she swiveled around to face him. Determination filled her. Determination and a strength she hadn't experienced in a long time. "I'm not interested in hearing about all that mate stuff." She held up a hand to silence him when he looked like he might speak. "If the invitation to hitch a ride with you to Ashtown is still open, I want to go. Today. *Now.*"

CHAPTER SIX

KADE WATCHED ALLY OUT OF THE CORNER OF HIS EYE, AS she drove them back to Tessa's. She obeyed the traffic laws to the letter, each movement slow and deliberate as she navigated Pepper's streets. As if taking her time would somehow solve whatever bothered her.

A bother she hadn't revealed to him. He opened his mouth, his wolf urging him to question her, but then snapped it closed just as quick. The harsh, grim set of her mouth stopped him from speaking. Whatever had made her change her mind about accompanying them to Ashtown, she clearly had no intention of sharing. At least not with him.

Yet.

But she would. Something had destroyed her trust in all things. He had no idea what happened to her, but he would work hard to earn her trust. His wolf growled, furious that their mate refused to recognize them immediately. He struggled to soothe the beast, assuring the wolf that they simply needed patience.

They would spend hours together finishing the packing. Hopefully by the time they were done, she would have come to her senses. He sensed her wolf just beneath the surface of her skin, her inner animal strong and ever-present inside her. Hopefully it wouldn't take her beast long to convince her that they were fated mates.

They found Tessa on the front porch when they returned. The older woman was rocking softly while reading a romance novel featuring a bare-chested hunk on the cover. More than he needed to know about Lucy's grandmother. Much more.

Ally didn't pull her little car into the garage, simply throwing it into park once they neared the house. She jumped out and hurried up the cobblestone path and Kade fought his body's response to the sight. Her lush curves jiggled as she rushed toward the home. Her ass bounced and swayed with her hurried steps and his palms tingled, fingertips aching as his wolf pushed forward. It wanted them to trace her curves, squeeze that plump ass, and explore every inch of her body.

He lost himself in that fantasy for a moment, desire for his mate flooding him.

At least until he noticed her behavior. The way her attention flicked from left to right and occasionally paused to stare into the deep shadows.

As if she searched for danger.

There was no reason for his mate to ever be fearful. Ever. Though he sensed that if he tried to command her not to be afraid, it wouldn't go over well.

"Tessa, why aren't you inside packing?" Ally's tone verged on worried.

"I've been packed for days," Tessa said, taking a long sip from a tall, sweating glass of lemonade that made Kade's mouth water. "At least, all my personals. You didn't think I'd let some stranger paw through my unmentionables, did you?"

The old woman let her gaze slide down the length of his body and back up again. "Of course, had I known he was going to look like *that*, I might have let him."

"Tessa!" Ally's blush turned her face a bright pink and even the tops of her ears reddened.

Kade couldn't decide if he should act amused or scandalized. Instead he settled on flirting with his alpha's grandmother-in-law and gave Tessa a slow wink that had the older woman giggling like a young girl.

"So, what's the plan, Stan?" Tessa said, still grinning at Kade. "I'm not in a hurry, but I'll be damned if I'll let you interrupt me once I get to the good part." Tessa waved the paperback in his direction. "Based on the number of times the heroine has sighed breathlessly, I'd say you have a chapter before the hero grips her with a passion unrivaled."

"I just need to pack my things and then we can go." Ally strode to the front door, hand resting on the old knob.

Tessa blinked up at her. "I thought you were staying?"

Ally glanced away, cheeks still pink, and he scented Ally's lie before it left her lips. "I changed my mind." She shrugged. "I miss Lucy."

A truth and yet a lie in one. Kade kept his mouth shut and let his mate have the lie.

"Hmm." Tessa let her gaze slide from Ally to Kade and then offered him a sly wink. "The more the merrier." She snapped her book closed. "Better get a move on, then."

Kade had taken advantage of Ally's distraction, closing the distance between them and pausing at the top of the steps. When it looked like Tessa was rising from her chair, he finished his walk to the front door.

He crowded Ally, bodies nearly touching, but not quite. Less than an inch separated them, but he still sensed her heat, the delicious warmth that stretched out for him. He reached past her and placed his hand atop hers, both of them grasping the knob.

Which earned him a fierce glare. "And *what* do you think you're doing?"

"Helping." He grinned. He couldn't help it. She was gorgeous all flushed—cheeks pink and eyes sparking with anger.

Ally jerked back. "Uh… No. Not so much."

"Why not? Afraid I'll *paw* through your unmentionables?" Kade couldn't help but tease her. He waggled his eyebrows and was pretty sure he caught the hint of a smile before she rolled her eyes and huffed at him.

"Among other things," she grumbled.

Kade shrugged. "The more hands on deck, the sooner we can get out of here. You tell me where to go and I'll do as I'm told."

Ally sighed and slipped her hand off the knob, giving him control so he could open the door. She slipped through the doorway as soon as she could and strode to a stack of empty boxes. She grabbed a couple and tossed them in his direction. "Do you promise to behave?"

"Fine, as long as you promise to behave."

Kade grinned but stayed silent. Hell no, he wasn't making that kind of promise. A wolf behave himself while he was so close to his mate?

Though that really wasn't the whole reason he kept his

lips sealed. She led him up the stairs, her full ass bouncing with every step, and he nearly swallowed his tongue at the sight. His teeth ached, fangs threatening to burst free, so he could nibble that plump ass. His cock hardened with the thought and he struggled against the soul deep need to pull her close.

That struggle grew even more difficult when they reached the top of the stairs and turned right... into her bedroom. Her sweet scent surrounded him, wrapping him in a blanket of utter calm and raging desire. The buttercream walls were a soft, soothing tone, the hue matched by the quilt that lay draped across the bed. A bright sprinkling of raspberry pink was interspersed with the soft yellow, making him think of a dessert he'd love to consume.

The rest of her room was mostly bare. A handful of built-in shelves lined the walls and where he would have expected cutesy knick-knacks and mementos, he found only a dozen books—nothing else. On the bedside table there was a single picture frame.

He glanced around the sparsely decorated room. "This shouldn't take too long."

Ally strode to the closet and hauled a duffle bag out, swinging it to thump onto the bed. "I like to live simply."

Kade suspected there was nothing "simple" about Ally's life, but kept his mouth shut.

"Can you pack up the books while I grab some of Lucy's

things?" She looked to him then, their gazes clashing, and he finally had a moment to truly *look* at her. A smile graced her lips, but tension lingered around her eyes. Her hands trembled, shaking so badly that she nearly dropped the box she held.

He reached out and gently took the cardboard from her hands.

"Of course, I can." He agreed to her request even as his body screamed not to let her out of sight.

He listened as she left him in her room, not moving until he heard her reach the other. Then he focused on his own task. The first stack of books snared his attention:

Wolves in North America

Howl: The History of Wolves and Their Migration Patterns

Taming the Beasts: A Year with the Wolves of Wyoming

Each had worn covers, multiple dog-eared pages, and even sticky notes poking out from random spots. Clearly Ally had read these books more than once, but Kade couldn't understand why. Did she have a thing for natural wolves? Surely, she wasn't studying them thinking it somehow translated to werewolf behavior.

Was she?

No, he shook his head. No natural-born werewolf would think such a thing.

Which brought him to another thought about werewolves. Where the hell was her pack? Lone wolves generally went feral without the support of a pack.

He was torn. On one hand, she wasn't feral by any means, though she did have a bit of grouch in her. That made him think she might have a pack near and yet her ever-ready go bag showed the lengths she would go to maintain her independence. His mate was a mystery, one he wanted to unravel. Soon. Learning her story was a bond-deep, driving need. A puzzle he needed to solve. Sometimes the best way to do that was to simply ask.

The creak of a floorboard let him know she was on her way back. She said nothing, simply went about packing up an array of creams and lotions from the top of her chest of drawers.

"So..." Kade kept one eye on her as he packed the remaining books, "you never mentioned the name of your pack."

Ally froze in place, eyes widening slightly, and she dropped the small vial in her hand. It slammed against the hardwood floor and shattered, filling the room with an overpowering smell of perfume. One that obliterated the most tempting flavor he had ever smelled—her natural scent.

"Shit," she muttered and dragged her gaze away from him. "I need to clean that up."

Dammit, he'd spooked her with a simple question. He sighed and let her scurry from the room. He didn't challenge her sudden retreat. He'd seen the wide-eyed fear in her expression after he'd asked the question. She'd panicked—terror overriding all else.

He did his best to ignore the pungent scent that filled the room and instead focused on adding things to his half-full box. A photo of Lucy and Ally, a pair of pink bunny slippers tucked under the bed, an Atlanta Falcons baseball hat. Moving to the dresser, he found the first drawer filled with every delicate thing he wanted to see but didn't dare touch. Not yet, anyway.

Lacy panties of every shape, size and color were scattered about the drawer. He couldn't help but imagine Ally wearing them and nothing else. Her body bared to him as he craved. His wolf rushed forward, pushed and prodding him. Not to be freed, but to do exactly as his mind desired. To do as Tessa suggested and let those bits of lace and silk slide through his fingers.

Kade shook his head. Digging through her panties wouldn't be right, but he couldn't let himself stand there staring at them much longer. He only had so much control.

He slammed the drawer shut just as Ally hurried into the room, paper towels in one hand and a spray bottle in the other. She made it two steps into the room before freezing in place and giving him a narrow-eyed stare.

"What are you doing?" A soft pink teased the apples of her cheeks.

Kade leaned against the dresser and quirked an eyebrow. "You've got some interesting things in there. One was particularly long and buzzy."

She snorted. "Liar. That's in my bedside table—"

Soft pink turned into an alarming shade of red with her confession and he couldn't help but let his mind wander. Couldn't help but imagine her naked and spread out before him, that toy buried between her thighs...

"I..." Ally wrenched her attention away and dropped to her knees beside the fragrant puddle, using paper towels to soak up the worst of the mess.

Kade went to her, kneeling at her side and carefully gathering the thin shards of glass. "Just so you know, once you accept that we're mates, you'll never have to use your little *friend* again. Though I wouldn't mind watching you."

Ally scrubbed the wood so hard he thought she might rub the countless years of sealer away until she reached bare wood.

"You also need to know that I know better than to touch anything without permission. I learned that lesson long ago. I'm a wolf that likes to eat."

In more ways than one, but he pulled his mind away from the gutter.

Ally jerked back and glared at him again. "What the hell is that supposed to mean?"

Kade couldn't help the grin that pulled at the corner of his lips or suppress the laughter that managed to escape. "Miss Rose, I think your mind might be in the gutter." He shook his head. "When I was just a pup, I got so bored one day that I went looking for something to do. Mason had just finished a diorama about the Wild West for school and left it on the dining room table in the middle of the pack house to let the glue dry." His smirk turned into a true grin, the memory bringing that smile to his face.

"Those little plastic cowboys and horses looked like fun, so I took them into the woods and pretended I was an outlaw." He squirted more cleaner and she silently wiped it away. She wouldn't look him in the eye, but he sensed she was listening. "I broke half of them and lost the rest in the forest. Now my father was my dad, but also the alpha of the pack, and he held us to a higher standard than other pups. We were the future for the pack. He taught me a very painful lesson about touching other people's belongings without asking."

Ally finally turned wide, worried eyes on him, lower lip trembling, and whispered when she spoke. "What happened?"

Kade shook his head ruefully. "I didn't get dessert for a *month*. Mom was one hell of a baker, too. She made cakes for *everyone* in the pack. I probably missed out on a dozen different birthday cakes."

Ally stared at him, eyes wide with surprise.

"What?" He furrowed his brow.

"That's it? That's all your father did to punish you?"

"That's not enough? Let me tell you, there isn't a worse punishment for a pup with a sweet tooth as big as mine."

She looked doubtful. "Seriously?"

It was his turn to frown. What kind of pack had she come from?

"How else would he have punished a pup? It's not like pups are beaten. Only sentries take physical punishment, and that's only because it's part of their training. When a sentry makes a mistake, his error can affect more than just him. It can affect the whole pack. You know better than anyone that wolves naturally want to please their alpha. Normally it doesn't take much to keep the little ones in line. Except when they're really, really bored, apparently," he drawled.

He chuckled softly to himself while Ally... Ally's expression became distant and unfocused, face growing pale while she lost herself in what he guessed were some dark thoughts. She obviously didn't believe a pup wouldn't be beaten for succumbing to the temptation of toys sitting right in front of him. If she thought that, no wonder she kept her distance from other wolves.

His beast snarled. It demanded they prove to her that he hadn't lied, but Kade reached out with a calming touch. He mentally stroked his beast's fur, fingers sinking into its coat. Now wasn't the time to push. Once they made it to Ashtown, he'd spend every minute of every day proving to her that whatever she'd experienced wasn't how a pack worked. At least, not in the Blackwood pack.

CHAPTER SEVEN

"ALLY, ARE YOU COMING?" KADE CALLED FROM DOWNSTAIRS, his too-sexy, rumbling voice wrapping around her, teasing her.

Ally growled and gritted her teeth, fighting her wolf's demand she hurry and get close to him already. She jammed the last few toiletries into her duffle and strode from the bathroom. Frustration rode her hard, her inner animal twitchy and snarling at all the scents in the house.

She'd spent the last two days surrounded by burly Blackwood werewolves, the males bustling around the house as they packed up the remainder of Tessa's forty years of memories. Sure, Tessa had handled the smaller things before the wolves arrived, but when the new guys showed, she'd put them to work with the heavy lifting. Then she'd sat back and watched, occasionally fanning herself.

Ally had caught Tessa flicking off the air conditioner more than once. The older woman hoped the heat would become too much for the men and they'd be forced to rip off their shirts. Ally had just sighed and turned the A/C back on. She'd heard Kade order the males to keep their hands to themselves and clothes on their bodies when around Ally. They'd end up passing out from heat stroke if Tessa kept playing games with the temperature.

"Ally…" Another shout from Kade and Ally rolled her eyes.

"I'm coming, I'm coming," she grumbled. He was the one who delayed their departure and *now* he was rushing her?

She'd been hoping to leave Pepper the day they'd met, but the moment Tessa discovered Ally was coming along, plans changed. Tessa decided she needed all of her furniture. Not for herself, but for Ally's new place in Ashtown.

Ally didn't have the heart to tell her that she wasn't sure how long she'd stick around.

But her demand had meant waiting for vans and movers. Not just any movers, either. Nah, more Blackwood werewolves showed up on Tessa's front porch.

Their presence left her feeling more exposed than ever. More vulnerable despite Kade's promise to protect her and care for her. On the other hand, she hadn't caught even a hint of Brian's scent since Kade arrived. She was grateful for that at least.

One thing she *wasn't* grateful for was how her wolf reacted to Kade. The horny beast exerted just enough control to somehow trick Ally into walking into whatever room he happened to be in. On one particularly steamy afternoon—one on which Tessa had conveniently turned off the AC—he'd whipped off his shirt, exposing his rippled abs, thick biceps and rock-solid pecs. Her wolf had surged, almost snatching control. Ally had managed to cling to her humanity by a thread. The ass had known exactly how he'd affected her too. As she'd turned to scurry out, she'd spied Kade's wide grin.

To his credit, he hadn't mentioned anything about being mates again. That didn't stop the idea from constantly filling her mind, though. All it would take was one hint of his laughter reaching her ears and then she'd find herself fantasizing about snuggling into those burly arms, being held and loved and protected…

And held down while Brian… Why was it that her fantasies always turned into nightmares? After all these years, why did Brian still have such control over her?

Ally skipped down the last few stairs and met Kade's gaze, his teasing grin forcing her to respond in kind.

"It's about time," he teased.

"Ha ha, very funny," she drawled blandly even though her

lips twitched. She brushed past him, her arm skimming his, and that woodsy essence caressed her. "Are you sure your guys can be trusted with Tessa's stuff? I have no idea where she's going to put it all, but God help the man who breaks a single Hummel."

"I've put the fear of the Alpha into them," he followed her outside. "I reminded them that Tessa is the Alpha Mate's grandmother, and if Gam-Gam ain't happy, Lucy won't be happy, which means Mason will be downright pissed off. If that doesn't scare them, nothing will."

Ally nodded and headed for her Focus. Tessa sat in the passenger seat, unfolding a huge map of Georgia. The old woman had yet to master the joys of smartphones. The car was packed with junk—almost all of it Tessa and Lucy's—as was Kade's SUV.

"Hey Tessa," Kade called, "are you sure you don't want to drive yourself? It's only a couple of hours."

Ally shot him a dark glare. The male was impossible. He'd been angling to ride with Ally back to Ashtown, but thankfully that was impossible. Tessa hadn't driven a car in over a decade and her license had expired long ago. They'd already decided Kade would follow the Focus, but of course he just had to try again. If he wasn't so annoying, Ally might have found his tenacity was charming.

"Only if you want me to end up dead in a ditch

somewhere," Tessa muttered. She was too distracted by trying to figure out where Pepper was on the map. Apparently even Triple-A thought it was too small to put on there.

Kade winked at Ally. "Can't blame a guy for trying!"

Her wolf growled and then whimpered, clawing at her to follow the big male. It not only wanted to jump in Kade's SUV, but also wanted to find out if the backseat was roomy enough for them both. Ally tried to remind it that, even if she did find him kind of cute—okay, hot—it was better to keep their distance. The more they were together, the easier she laughed and the safer she felt. Safe enough to relax a little, but that sure as hell wasn't smart. Brian would take advantage of any weakness or lapse. Her life depended on remaining hyper-vigilant.

Unfortunately, Kade's easy smile had a way of making her feel tingly all over. The tingles always started in her tummy, then radiated out in every direction—especially down. When his shoulder brushed against her back as he passed behind her to head to his SUV, Ally's vision went topsy-turvy, and her feet tangled up on each other.

One second she was walking toward her car, the next she was airborne and headed for an epic face-plant. Instead of a mouthful of broken teeth, her body was encircled by warm skin and solid muscle, cradling and protecting her. Somehow, he'd caught her before she hit the ground, and now he carried her in his arms like a hero in a fairy tale.

Desire hit her hard, thick and fast. She scented the warm musk of it in the air around them, clouding over every other scent. Not just her own need, either. The dark look in Kade's eyes told her it had struck him the same way. Then he blinked and swallowed hard, before setting her back on her feet.

She hissed and groaned the moment her right foot touched ground. "*Ow.*"

"Are you okay?" Concern filled his eyes.

"I'm fine." She rotated her ankle and tried not to wince at the pain. "See?"

He grunted and scooped her into his arms again. He carried her to the porch and lowered her to the steps, then lifted her leg, so he could have a better look. Callused fingertips ghosted over her skin, the rough scratch teasing her nerves. What would it feel like to have his hands all over her body?

"It's just sprained." She pulled her foot from his hands. "It'll be fine in no time."

Another grunt. "You can't drive until it's healed."

She rolled her eyes. "If you're just trying to finagle a way to be alone with me for hours, you can forget it."

Her wolf howled its objection because the animal was *all over* being locked up in a car with Kade for hours. *Horn dog.*

"Are you okay, Ally?" Tessa hurried up the walkway. "That could have been a nasty tumble, sweetheart."

"She twisted her right ankle," Kade explained.

"I'm fine." Ally braced a hand on Kade's shoulder and used him to steady herself as she pushed herself upright. "Let's get going."

Ally gritted her teeth and put her foot on the next step. Pain shot up her leg, along her spine, and right out the top of her head. She managed to stay silent, but that hadn't been enough for Tessa. Why the hell couldn't she have been a better actor? *Why?*

"Oh, I don't think so little miss." Tessa shook her head. "I don't drive because I have common sense."

"And because you like to stare at Bobby Thompson when he drives you around town."

Tessa ignored her even though Ally *was* right. "Enough sense to stop you so that I don't die in a fiery wreck."

Tessa peered past Ally and into the house. Ally followed the older woman's line of sight and watched a shirtless wolf named Austin single-handedly carry a grandfather clock across the room. His muscles bulged, and his body was slick with sweat, accentuating his heavily carved muscles. The wolf was almost as sexy as Kade. Almost.

Ugh. What was wrong with her? Kade wasn't sexy. Werewolves weren't sexy. They were dangerous and evil.

"I'm sure one of Kade's fine young friends won't mind chauffeuring me around, isn't that right, Kade?" She shot Kade a grin and then resumed her perusal of the man-meat prowling through the house.

Kade chuckled. "I don't think he'll mind at all."

She was pretty sure Austin would mind being stuck in a car for hours with a flirty, occasionally handsy woman, but it didn't look like he'd have a choice.

Much like her. Being clumsy pushed her into this situation. She wanted to argue with him more, but it would be stupid to try to drive with her ankle screaming so loudly. Maybe if she had a few hours to heal… Nah, no sense in waiting. She'd been chomping at the bit to leave town and she wasn't going to waste another minute.

"Fine," she sighed, and turned to face Kade. "But don't get any bright ideas about carrying me around. I'm not an invalid. I can—"

He ignored her completely. He scooped her into his arms and carried her to the SUV, gently placing her in the passenger seat. He nudged the door closed and then retraced his path to the house. Probably to let Austin know about his new job. Ally's chest constricted, tightening more and more the greater the distance that separated them.

Nah, that was all in her mind. He wasn't affecting her physically. It was just a case of blue ovaries. She tugged on the handle and the door opened slightly so she could shout at the retreating wolf. "Bet you're pretty happy with yourself."

He spun around, big grin already plastered on his face, and spread his arms wide. His shirt pulled tight across his chest, the fabric outlining his toned body. "More than you can imagine!"

Within ten minutes, they were on the road. It took another fifteen to hit the highway and merge with traffic. Ally kept her visor pulled down, using the embedded makeup mirror to keep an eye on the Focus behind them. Tessa was waving her arms around, mouth going a mile a minute while she talked with a dazed Austin. Poor little werewolf.

Attention split between Tessa and Kade, she finally broke the quiet in the SUV. "So, tell me a little more about Ashtown?"

"It's the best place to live on Earth."

"Travelled a lot, have we?" She pulled her gaze from Tessa and quirked a single brow.

"Nope." He shook his head. "Don't have to when you live in the best place on Earth."

She rolled her eyes. "If you have nothing to compare it to, how do you know it's the best?"

"You don't have to visit every corner of the world to

appreciate where you are. It's the people who make a place, know what I mean?"

Ally turned to look at the lush scenery speeding past. "Not really, no."

Everything fell quiet. The silence was only broken by the thump of tires on asphalt. She glanced in the passenger side mirror at the traffic behind them and wondered if she'd ever get to stay in one place long enough to truly discover its people. Pepper had been her longest stay ever since Brian had entered her life. Then destroyed it.

"All I can say is that Ashtown has everything a small town should. There's a coffee shop called Beans and it's the hub of town gossip. Dickey's is the best little greasy spoon in all of Georgia. Then, of course," he shot her a wide smile. "there's my family."

Ally's heart gave a little stab, but she tried to sound unmoved. "Yeah?"

"Yeah. My brothers are great. Though Mason's been a little on edge ever since Ghost Kitty came into his life."

"Ghost Kitty?"

Kade barked out a laugh. "I was sure Lucy would have told you about that damned cat. Ghost Kitty had a litter of kittens under Lucy's old porch. When she moved into the Blackwood pack house, she insisted on giving them a home. Since Mason can't say no to Lucy, he's got a herd of cats racing around the house and destroying everything they can with their little claws and sharp assed teeth." He stopped and looked her way, his head tilted. "Is that what you call a group of cats? A herd?"

"Glaring."

"Who?"

"What?"

"Who's glaring?"

Ally laughed. "No, a group of cats is called a *glaring*."

"Oh," Kade paused for a moment then jerked his head in a brisk nod. "Sounds about right with those little assholes."

Ally couldn't help giggle at that.

"Anyway," he continued, "Mason found a kitten in his shoe the other day and it scared him half to death."

Ally laughed outright. "The Alpha was scared of a kitten? I don't believe you! You've got to be lying."

"I swear!"

Never in a million years had she expected to ever laugh with another werewolf. She couldn't help wondering how a werewolf pack could be so... lighthearted. After everything that happened with Brian, she never imagined such a thing was possible. Maybe it wasn't. Maybe Kade was a far better actor than her.

"So, Lucy's happy?" she asked.

"Ridiculously happy, as far as I can tell. I've never seen anybody fit in with the pack so fast. She's going to be a fantastic Alpha Mate. Everyone loves her."

Ally glanced at the traffic behind them again, trying to find the right way to ask a question that had been nagging her for days. His brief explanation of how Lucy had been changed into a werewolf seemed sketchy. If she'd been turned against her will, Ally would make it her mission in life to get her and Tessa the hell out of Ashtown immediately. They could be sisters on the run, a pack of their own with a sassy, elderly human mascot.

"Can you tell me more about how Lucy was turned?"

"I'll tell you what I know. It was actually a lucky break, if you think about it. The accidental bite from the pup is what led Mason to her."

Ally snorted. Getting bitten and turned into a werewolf was lucky? Finding her supposed "mate" was lucky? "Uh-huh."

Kade's brow pulled down in a frown. "If little Charlie hadn't bitten her, Mason would never have found her. He would have gone feral and… we would have had to put him down."

Maybe that *would have been luckiest of all.* The bitter thought flowed through her mind.

His voice was low and soft, no hint of the teasing male from moments ago. "I know you don't like talking about it, but Lucy and Mason are fated mates. Because of that, he was able to claim her and ease her transition. If he hadn't, she probably would have died."

She whipped her head around to stare at him—eyes wide as shock slapped her and alarm made her heard race. Her best friend had almost died, and Ally hadn't been there. "*What?*"

He looked confused. "She was bitten by someone who wasn't her mate. That's almost always deadly to humans, you know that."

No, she didn't, but she kept that to herself. She stayed silent and fought to control her breathing as he explained that something called the "National Ruling Circle" had investigated Lucy's change and cleared the Blackwood pack of any wrongdoing. Her heart rate picked up to a breakneck speed and she pressed her hand to her chest. A fine bead of sweat gathered on her upper lip as her panic continued to rise. She closed her eyes and pushed her painful memories down to the depths of Hell where they'd been born. Her wolf whimpered pitifully.

"Does she know about me? That I'm…"

"A werewolf?" Kade asked. "No, that's your secret to share."

Ally wasn't sure whether she should thank him or curse

him. If he'd blabbed to Lucy, she wouldn't have to admit she'd been lying to the most wonderful and generous people she'd ever known.

With a heavy sigh, Ally let her gaze drift to the makeup mirror again. Tessa was still jabbering, and Austin still looked shell-shocked, but he kept a comfortable distance between the vehicles, so Tessa was safe enough.

A few cars behind the nondescript Focus, a red sedan eased a few feet onto the shoulder before slowly pulling back into its lane. It hadn't concerned her at first. Probably just someone toying with their cell phone which was *such* a smart thing to do while doing eighty miles an hour. But then they'd done it again. And again.

Okay, maybe not a phone jockey. Was the driver drunk this early in the day? They weren't going slow and the highway wasn't crowded. It wasn't like they were hogging any lanes or dragging their ass. What the hell?

Kade moved from the middle lane to the right and she made sure Austin followed suit. But he wasn't the only one. The red sedan kept right on Austin's ass.

That red…

A memory prodded her mind, pushing and shoving itself forward. She closed her eyes and let it flow through her. A red car with tinted windows. Idling in the middle of the street. A shifted Kade injured and unconscious. Then the stink of Brian as the car raced off.

She swallowed hard and pressed her hand to her stomach, praying her breakfast would stay put. Nausea swept over her and saliva pooled in her mouth, the urge to vomit increasing with every breath.

She glanced in the mirror again, praying she was wrong but knowing she was right. The car that followed them was the same one that had run Kade down. The one that'd been drenched in Brian's sticky scent. She couldn't make out the driver's face, but she knew who sat behind the wheel.

"You know, Tessa's safe with Austin." Kade must have scented her distress but hadn't interpreted the cause correctly. "He's a good wolf and a good driver. If he knows what's good for him, he'll take care of your car, too."

"Okay." She forced a smile and tried for a casual tone. "So... I don't suppose your guys finished early and already hit the road, did they?"

Kade frowned. "No. They have at least another day's work ahead of them. Possibly more since they're a man short now. Why?"

She nibbled her lower lip. Of course, he'd have to ask why!

"No reason." She shrugged. "I just thought I saw someone following us and wondered if they caught up to us."

"No reason?" Kade's demeanor changed, the smiling man replaced by a dark hardness. His gaze locked onto the rearview mirror, an occasional glance flicking to the road in front of them before returning to his search.

"Right. No reason," Ally insisted. The scent of Kade's suspicion drifted over her while at the same time, he hit the gas a little harder.

CHAPTER EIGHT

ALLY'S ANXIETY HUNG IN THE AIR LIKE A HEAVY FOG, sending his wolf into a protective frenzy. He wanted to get his hands on whoever was making her feel so fearful just as much as his beast, but she wasn't giving up any details.

He pressed a button on the SUV's steering wheel and told his vehicle to call Austin. It only took one ring for the other wolf to answer.

"Hey Kade!"

Austin's voice boomed out of the SUV's speakers. He sounded a little too happy to talk to someone other than Tessa, which would have given Kade a chuckle if he hadn't been so focused on their current situation.

"Pull off at the next rest stop in a half-mile."

"Are we swapping drivers?" Austin sounded happy at the idea.

Kade could almost smell the poor guy's desperation. "'Fraid not, brother."

There was a sigh, followed by a grumbled "okay," and then the call disconnected.

As soon as Austin hung up, Ally turned to him. "Why are we stopping? We've only been on the road a few minutes."

"Which one is it?"

She acted puzzled by his question. "Huh? One what?"

"Which car is tailing us? The black Crown Vic?"

"I don't know what you're talking about." She continued with the charade even as a red flush crept up her chest all the way to her hairline.

"Or is it the red Accord?"

Her eyes nearly popped out of her head and the stink of her fear increased, which pushed his wolf closer to the edge of his control. To the animal, protecting its mate from whatever caused her fear included fangs and claws. It didn't care that a wolf couldn't drive a car. It simply knew that Ally should never fear anything or anyone.

"Ally, I can smell your anxiety and I can sure as hell smell your lies."

Without another word, he pulled off at the next exit, Austin dutifully following along. He pulled into the first available spot and threw the SUV into park.

"Stay put," he instructed as he jumped out.

And dammit, he should have known she wouldn't listen. Her constant refusal to blindly obey him turned him on, but it also frustrated the hell out of him. Though he couldn't deny his wolf settled the moment she limped to his side at the back of the SUV. The two of them watching the traffic speed past.

The tension between them crackled and sparked, and he soon found her delicate hand wiggling into his grip. He gave her a reassuring squeeze as the red car he'd suspected blew past the rest stop exit. Air whooshed out of Ally's pursed lips and her shoulders curled forward.

"See? It was nothing." She flashed him a fragile smile.

He stared at her, wishing she'd open up and tell him what the hell was wrong. *Wish in one hand, shit in the other and see which one fills up first.* It was clear he'd have to take matters into his own hands if he wanted to find out what had frightened her so much.

Austin had just clambered out of the Focus and was stretching his back when Kade pulled Ally toward a grassy patch.

"Austin, stay here and keep your eyes peeled for a red Accord. Ally and I need to have a conversation."

He kept hold of her hand and pulled her along. While she wasn't kicking and screaming, her resistance grew the nearer they walked to an empty picnic table. The moment they were close enough, he released her hand and gripped her waist. She was such a tiny little thing. Curves in all the right places, but still small compared to him. Delicate. Vulnerable. With her on the table, they were now eye-to-eye—no hiding for his mate.

A couple of kids walked a dog nearby, and travelers traipsed past them to reach the restrooms. Not the most private spot in the world, but it'd do.

Leaning in so close he could smell her shampoo, he dropped his hands to rest on the wood on either side of her hips. He yearned to grab those hips and pull her close, but he needed answers first. His wolf growled at the delay in claiming their mate but was soothed by her nearness. For now.

"No more games, understand?" He stared into her warm brown eyes.

She lifted her head and stared down her nose at him. "I have no idea what you're talking about."

"Uh-huh. Why did you think someone was following us?"

Ally shrugged. "I guess I watch too many cop shows."

"Who was in the red car?"

"What red car?" Oh, she had that innocent look down but that would only work on a human. Wolves had a sense of smell that easily revealed lies.

"Enough with the bullshit, Ally." He tried to keep his voice low, but apparently didn't do a very good job. A mother leading her child to the bathroom shot him a glare.

Ally's defiant gaze turned to her lap. She fidgeted, twisting and twining her fingers. She gnawed on her bottom lip, and the air of anxiety she'd held since her first moments with him dissipated into something more like briny, bitter sadness.

"Please tell me what's going on." He was less gruff this time, but she still refused to meet his gaze. Instead, her eyes drifted toward the traffic rushing by and lost focus.

"Do you have anything from your past that hurts so much that to remember it— just *remember* it—makes you feel like you'll die from the pain?" The words were hardly more than a harsh whisper.

He edged backward, unsure how to answer her. The short answer, of course, was no. The deaths of his parents came close, but not to the extreme she described. But his answer wasn't important here—only hers mattered.

"When your only method of self-preservation is to forget or risk going insane?"

At last, her gaze locked onto his. A shiver of anticipation raised the hairs on the back of his neck and his wolf paced inside him.

"You wanted to know where my pack was, but the thing is, I don't have one." A single tear escaped her eyes and traced a damp path down her cheek. "I haven't gone feral because I've pushed the pain so far down inside myself that it's hidden in a dark crevice. A place just for that agony to live. Understand?"

Kade could do nothing but tell the truth. "No. But I want to." He reached for her, gently rubbing her arm as he spoke. "I want to help you—I *need* to help you—but you need to trust me."

"Trust you?" She snorted, and another tear escaped. She dashed it away before speaking again. "I don't even know you."

Tears still sparkled in her eyes, but she didn't look away when he moved closer. He leaned into her space, pressing his forehead to hers. His wolf allowed him to hear her heartbeat, listen as it slowed until it thrummed in time with his own. Soon, what remained of her anxiety drifted away on the warm breeze, leaving him surrounded by the sweetness of her natural scent.

"I will be your shield," he whispered, "if you'll let me. I'll protect you from whatever is haunting you. I'll protect you from *everything*—past, present and future. Let me."

The tension in her shoulders eased and she leaned into him, adjusting her position until she was able to nuzzle his cheek. Not a lot, just a little, but it was enough for now. Her breathing slowed and shallowed to match his. He knew that if he cupped her cheek, she would allow his lips to meet her own.

As much as he craved a taste of her lips, and despite his wolf's demands, he refused to rush her. Her past still clouded her, chased her and nipped at her heels. It was what stopped her from recognizing their bond and he refused to rush her. Eventually she would no longer be able to deny the powerful draw between them, he simply had to be patient. In that moment, it was enough to be close to her, to share her burden—as much as she'd let him, anyway.

"You need to know something, Ally. There's nothing —*nothing*—I wouldn't do for you. Your soul knows even if your brain won't accept the truth, and that's okay." He placed his palm to her chest. "As long as you know it in here."

Her warm breath fanned his cheek and he smiled to himself, only to be interrupted by a loud cackle. The quiet, touching moment broken, they both swung their attention to the parked cars. Tessa sat perched on the hood of Ally's car, slapping her knee and pointing at a red-faced Austin.

"Oh God," Ally sighed. "She probably told him one of her stories."

"Austin is a seasoned warrior, one of our very best. What could such a sweet little old lady have said that would make him blush?"

Ally smirked. "Trust me, you do *not* want to know."

He scoffed. "I think I can handle it."

"Don't say I didn't warn you. It was probably the one about her passionate threesome with JFK and Marilyn Monroe. Or maybe it was about the time she snorted cocaine off Dean Martin's dick. Or it could have been—"

"Stop!" Kade's eyes widened as his stomach heaved. "You were right. I don't want to know."

CHAPTER NINE

THE REMAINDER OF THE JOURNEY WAS A MARKED improvement over the first half hour—of course, probably not for poor Austin who'd still been stuck in a car with Tessa. Tessa who had an endless supply of dirty stories to share.

Ally had kept an eye out for a red Accord for the rest of the trip even though Kade probably watched as well. Their luck had held, and they hadn't seen the car again. She was free. At least for now. She wasn't so naive as to think Kade would drop the subject of their mysterious tail, but for now, he was giving her the time she needed. Now all she had to worry about was telling her best friend her deepest, darkest secret.

With the sun just disappearing beneath the horizon, the street lights flickered on to greet the coming night. A sky full of pinks and purples dimmed with each passing second. Ally sank deeper into her seat, as if that and the night could hide her from what lay ahead.

Kade shot her a curious glance. "We still have a bit."

She scooted up, not wanting to let too much of her anxiety show, even if he could smell it all over her. "Any suggestions on how to pass the time?"

He offered her a mischievous smile, one that held both a hint of teasing and desire. She held up a hand. "Never mind. Forget I asked."

"Someone has their mind in the gutter," he teased. "I was going to say we could get to know each other a little better. I ask a question, you answer, and then ask me whatever you want."

That sounded like a *terrible* idea. "I don't know…"

"Tell you what. You can even pass on any questions that you're uncomfortable with."

Ally hesitated, but finally agreed. *I'm going to regret this.* "Okay."

"You don't have a Georgia accent. Where are you from, Miss Rose?"

"Pass."

Kade laughed. "So soon?"

"Hey, either you make these passes easy for me to use or

we sit in silence."

Kade sighed. "Fine, fine. Do you have any siblings?"

"Pass."

"Are you messing with me?"

"No, just ask less personal questions." She squirmed. "Why don't you try, I don't know, ask what my favorite cartoon was when I was little?"

"Okay, what was it?"

"The Powerpuff Girls."

Kade rolled his eyes. "Yeah, that tells me *worlds* about you."

"Fine, fine." She grumbled and then sighed. "Something more personal, but not *too* personal is that I love grocery stores."

"Yeah, that's not weird."

Ally laughed. "Hear me out. As a teen, I worked in the produce department of a local grocery store. I loved it. Making the displays pretty really appealed to me. Now I love checking out the layouts of stores wherever I visit. Especially the fancy-schmancy gourmet stores. You wouldn't believe some of the bizarre fruits and veggies I've discovered."

"I suppose that counts as personal. You must enjoy cooking then."

"When I get the chance. Which I didn't get much while living with Tessa and Lucy. I'm not as talented as my s—"

She caught herself before admitting her sister was the chef of the family. Clearing her throat, she turned the tables on him.

"What about you, Mr. Big Bad Wolf?"

His eyebrow shot up as he cast a heated look in her direction. He growled low in his throat and the sensation sizzled throughout her body. "I could get used to hearing that from you."

"Quit trying to distract me," she pressed. "Spill."

He smirked and turned back to the road, then pressed a finger against his nose.

Laughing, she shook her head at the odd wolf. "What are you doing?"

"Thinking."

"I've never seen anyone think like that."

"Then you've never seen anyone do it correctly," he shot back. "Now, about me. I do like to cook, but I mostly like to do it with things I find."

"Like roadkill?"

"No," he laughed with her. "It'll probably make sense when you see just how much land we have, but my parents and grandparents taught us all from an early age how to live off the land. My dad would take us fishing in the streams and my grandmother would make salads from the local vegetation. I can't tell you how many times she took me to pick honeysuckle."

Ally smiled. "A real down-home Georgia boy."

"That's me."

"By 'us', you mean you and your brother Mason?"

"And our younger brother, Gavin. He's the pack enforcer."

Ally did her best to ignore the chill that rippled down her spine at the mention of a pack enforcer. Her experiences with them had never been what anyone would call positive, but she was committed to keeping an open mind about the Blackwood pack. If Kade was any indicator, maybe the Blackwood wolves wouldn't be too terrible…

"…Lucy?" The end of his question brought her back to the present.

"What about her?"

"You two seem as close as sisters, but you're still worried?"

Ally knew better than to think it was a question.

"I need to get better at hiding my feelings," she muttered.

"Or you could be even more open with them and share your thoughts with your mate," he suggested gently.

Kade turned off the highway and onto the rocky forest road. They were getting close. Civilization had been left behind and now trees loomed over them from every direction. Ally used the cover of darkness to let her true concern show by worrying her bottom lip and clenching her hands into fists.

Kade reached over and gave one fist a squeeze. "We'll be there soon. Might as well get it out now."

Ally loosened her fist and entwined hers with his. She took a deep breath and shared more of herself than she'd ever imagined she would. And it felt so easy and natural with him.

"It's just that I've been lying to her for so long. I know she'll feel hurt and I can't blame her. It's not like I can even break the news gently. The second she gets close to me, she'll smell my wolf. She's going to have so many questions, ones I can't answer."

He squeezed her fingers again, and she took that boost of strength. "Maybe, but Lucy is a wolf, too. She knows the importance of secrecy. I think you need to give her a little more credit. She might be surprised, but she'll still love you."

"I hope so."

The warmth of Kade's hand disappeared as he pulled up to an absolutely massive log cabin-style house. For a moment she wanted to reach out and snatch his hand back. To rest their joined hands in her lap and keep them there. Especially when a solitary light near the front door flicked on, revealing that someone was watching for them.

"Family forgives. Family understands," Kade murmured as he popped the SUV into park.

The front door opened, and two people walked out into the dim light. Ally immediately recognized the curvy figure of her bestie, and assumed the tall, burly dude next to her was Mason. As much as Ally wanted to run to Lucy, to throw herself into her arms and hug her to death, she couldn't will her fingers to grab the door handle.

Lucy waved.

Ally didn't budge.

Lucy glared and jammed her hands onto her hips.

Ally wasn't afraid of that glare. She was more afraid of never being on the receiving end again once Lucy knew about her lies.

Lucy held her hands up to her mouth. "Hurry up, Ally," she shouted, her voice reminding Ally of Tessa's, only more youthful. "Get your scaredy-cat ass out of that—"

Lucy stopped short, howling as the door bumped open wide and a white cat darted outside, followed by a herd— not a herd, a *glaring*—of kittens.

"Ghosty, not again!" Lucy cried.

The door banged open once more and a small boy scuttled past the adults, his hands outstretched as he chased the cats.

"Charlie!" Lucy shouted, but the boy was more focused on the kitties than obeying his elders.

The kittens darted between the boy's feet, drawing delighted squeals from him. Lucy and Mason ran down the steps to help him collect the wayward pets. Ally took advantage of the diversion to haul her "scaredy-cat ass" out of the SUV and join Kade near the bumper.

When the white mama cat—Ghost Kitty, no doubt—ran toward them, Ally kneeled down and held her hands out. Ghosty skidded to a stop and arched her back. Her tail fluffed out and she hissed ferociously. Ally was more familiar with dogs, but she knew cats well enough to know when one was about to protect her brood.

"No, wait," Ally stuttered, then jumped upright.

She scuttled one way, then the other, then backed around in a half-circle, trying to evade Ghosty's razor-sharp claws. She heard the others laughing, but she kept her focus on the pissed-off pussy. When Ghost Kitty launched her little body toward Ally—claws and teeth in full view— Ally lurched sideways and smack into a stone wall.

To her surprise, the wall tumbled to the ground along with her. Then its arms and legs got tangled up in hers. *What the hell had she run into?*

Lucy scooped up the demon cat and scolded it for being so bitchy, while Kade rushed toward them, growling in anger over something. Tessa's gleeful cackles could be heard all the way from the front seat of the Focus. And kittens scampered all around them.

"Oof," said a voice—a very male voice—connected to the legs and arms she was disentangling herself from.

Oh God. Mason.

Ally's body went cold with fear. She'd knocked over the leader of the pack, the Alpha. If she'd learned anything about crossing men like him, he was going to make her pay.

Scrambling to her feet, Ally blurted out one apology after another, her eyes glued to the ground. "I'm so sorry! Please forgive my clumsiness! It'll never happen again!"

She watched Mason using her peripheral vision and with every apology, Mason's brow pulled down more and more. Apologizing wasn't enough for this Alpha. She'd have to do something she'd promised she'd never do again. Funny how quickly pride got thrown out the window when faced with certain torture—if not death.

Body flooded with terror and quaking as she cowered in front of Mason, Ally pulled her hair to one side. She bowed her head and tipped it to the side, baring her neck for punishment. Then she waited. In truth, the waiting was worse than the punishment itself—usually. Brian used to delight in making her stand there for hours, forcing her to wallow in the uncertainty of her surviving whatever torture he'd dreamed up. Usually, by the time he decided to put her out of her misery, she almost wished he would. Permanently.

Tears dripped into the dirt at her feet. She hated this more than anything, and it was exactly what she'd been afraid would happen. It was exactly why she'd escaped Brian's pack of thugs to begin with.

She shouldn't have come, shouldn't have allowed herself to think she could live within another pack again. If she had an ounce of self-respect, she would have run and taken her chances in an unfamiliar forest. But with an Alpha looming over her, her wolf instincts kicked in. She was helpless to save herself from whatever punishment Mason decided to dole out.

But nothing happened. Only silence.

Daring to glance up at him through a curtain of hair, she caught his expression of utter confusion. When she tilted her head to expose more flesh, understanding flashed in his widening eyes.

He opened his mouth to speak, but a tiny finger poked her hip and drew their attention. Charlie, the cat-obsessed pup, grinned up at her and blurted out the secret she'd held tightly for so many years. "Hey! You're a werewolf too!"

CHAPTER TEN

Kade gripped Ally's shoulder, no longer able to watch her prostrating herself before his brother. She followed his touch willingly, allowing him to pull her into his embrace. Once she was fully in his arms, he rubbed her shaking arms and smoothed her hair, trying anything and everything he could to soothe her.

Fuck. He should have known wolves had abused her in the past. Her skittishness, her self-imposed exile from her own kind, and her fear of other packs were huge red flags. Ones he'd ignored. He'd been so distracted by the fact he'd found his mate in this beautiful, amazing woman, he hadn't put it together until he watched her submissive display and smelled her terror.

Whoever had harmed her had been a dominant werewolf and Kade's beast growled low as it imagined ripping the throat out of the asshole who'd hurt her. Since he had no way of seeking retribution at that moment, he settled for glaring at his brother.

Mason shrugged, and though Kade knew his brother had done nothing wrong, anger still rode him hard. Then there was a lingering resentment and fury that his brother had come into contact with Ally. Grinning like the asshole big brother he was, Mason winked at him. Of course, the Alpha would sense the connection between Kade and Ally.

So why couldn't Ally?

Glancing down at her, Kade tucked a strand of loose dark hair behind her ear and cupped her cheek. She leaned into his touch, nuzzling his palm. But no sooner had Ally relaxed, she tensed as the space around them erupted into noise and chaos again.

Lucy was the first to wade into the fray, peppering Ally with questions. "Are you kidding me? Is it true?" She sniffed the air. "I smell Kade and Mason. Charlie. And… Oh shit, I smell you!"

Kade had half a mind to hide Ally from Lucy and her intrusive questions, but he had no business coming between them. Besides, maybe she'd admit more about her past to her friend than she had to him.

"How did this happen? How long have you been like this? Have you always been? Where's your pack?" Lucy shook her head again, her eyes growing wider now. "There's just so much to cover. Seriously, what the fuck?"

Ally opened her mouth but didn't bother to answer. No one would be able to hear her. He'd barely been able to make out Lucy's incessant questioning, but only because he was used to the racket.

After the initial shocked silence in the group, Charlie had happily gone back to chasing kittens, squealing and throwing himself into nearby bushes and generally being a rambunctious pup. Meanwhile, Ghost Kitty had escaped Lucy's clutches and was delighting in circling Mason's legs.

"Could someone get out here and corral these damned cats already?" Kade shouted over his shoulder toward the pack house.

If that wasn't enough, car doors slammed behind them as Tessa and Austin joined the party.

"Excuse my French," The old woman stuffed her hands onto her hips and glared at each of them in turn. "Could someone please tell me what the fuck is going on? Werewolves?"

Ally trembled harder and buried her face in Kade's neck, avoiding Tessa's penetrating gaze. Enough was enough. Covering Ally's exposed ear with one hand, he let out a shrill whistle that silenced everyone. Mason cocked an eyebrow but allowed him to have his say.

"I think it's time we take this party inside and get some things straightened out," he said, giving Ally a gentle squeeze as he spoke. "Austin, help Charlie gather up the cats."

Austin grinned, probably thrilled to no longer be Tessa's escort. Mason moved to help the old woman up the porch steps, but she yanked her arm away and gave him an imperious glare.

"Do you think I'm made of porcelain? I've been climbing stairs since before your *daddy* was potty trained!"

Kade winced, but Mason laughed and apologized for being so presumptuous. Still, he was careful to follow behind the old woman as she mounted the steps slowly. Lucy shot Ally an appraising look before following along. Kade kept a protective arm around Ally while he guided her up the steps and into the Blackwood pack house.

Once inside the massive great room, they all settled on several plush couches. When Ally moved to sit at his side, Kade pulled her onto his lap. After the emotional day she'd had—not to mention everything she'd been through in her past—he needed to show her that he was her protector now. She would always be safe in his arms. Even an inch of space between them was too much for him to bear. She stiffened against him for a moment, then settled into his hold, the last remnants of fear dissipating.

Tessa flopped into a cozy armchair and kicked her feet up onto an old steamer trunk-turned coffee table. Her gaze bounced between Lucy and Ally for a moment, then cleared her throat.

"Now, would one of you ladies please enlighten me? Is this some kind of kinky cosplay retreat? I saw a special on those people who dress up as horses."

"Grandma!" Lucy gasped, no doubt as shocked as everyone else in the room that such a sweet, Southern granny would know cosplay and kink.

"What? I watch TV!"

Lucy hid her face for a moment, then met her grandmother's curious gaze. "Grandma, what I'm about to tell you is going to shock you and you won't want to believe me, but I promise I'm telling you the truth. We all are. We're—" she shot Ally a look, "—werewolves."

Tessa narrowed her gaze, then sucked on her teeth. "Go on."

Her nonplussed reaction confused Lucy. "Well, um…uh…"

"Never say 'um', dear. It makes you appear dull-witted."

Lucy blinked several times and then launched into her story. Ally tensed as Lucy related Charlie's accidental bite and the pain she suffered until Mason claimed her as his mate, which helped her transition. Throughout it all, Tessa sat expressionless as she listened, but at the last comment, she shook her head.

"I don't understand."

Mason jumped in. "Only fated mates can change humans into werewolves without a high risk of killing them. It was just sheer luck we were fated for each other and I found her in time, or else…"

No one needed further explanation of what might have happened.

Tessa quirked her wrinkled lips, then assessed Kade and Ally. "But it's not just Lucy and Mason. You're both werewolves too?"

Kade smiled proudly while Ally nodded miserably. His heart ached because she hated being a werewolf, and he vowed to do everything in his power to change her mind.

"Once Lucy's transformation was complete," Mason quickly added, "she was perfectly healthy. And happy. Right?"

Lucy stretched up and kissed his cheek. "Deliriously."

Mason looked as if he might lay her back on the couch and take her in front of everyone, but he managed to control himself. Kade might have laughed at him in the past, but now that he had Ally—her lush ass in his lap—he understood the level of his brother's strength. And the depth of his love for his mate.

Clearing his throat as he pulled a pillow onto his lap, Mason turned back to Tessa. "I want you to know that even though you're human, you are perfectly safe here with us. Probably safer than anywhere else on the planet."

Tessa snorted. "Of course, I am. My granddaughter would kick your ass if you so much as looked at me the wrong way."

Mason chuckled and grinned. "You're right about that."

Lucy moved from the couch and kneeled at her grandmother's feet, covering the woman's frail hand with both of hers. "I'm sorry to spring it on you like this, Grandma. We don't mean to shock you, but I didn't want a day to pass without telling you the truth. Do you have any questions?"

"There is one thing," Tessa said, stroking Lucy's cheek with an expression of deep love in her eyes.

"What? You can ask me anything."

Everyone held their breath, waiting for Tessa to ask one of them to shift as proof. Kade worried that seeing such a display might send the woman into cardiac arrest and struggled to think of the easiest way to prove themselves. But the question she asked shocked him more than her supposed affair with JFK.

"Do werewolves roll in their own shit like dogs?"

The room fell silent for a beat, then everyone—even Ally —broke into gales of laughter. Tears streamed down their faces while Tessa smiled serenely. Then, before Kade even knew what was happening, Lucy pulled Ally from him and into a ferocious hug.

The moment she left his lap, a part of him went with her, but he wasn't about to yank her away from her best friend. She'd been so worried about Lucy's reaction, and she needed the reassurance that nothing could break their bond.

"Man, I needed that," Lucy said when they finally broke apart. "I missed you."

Tears streaked Ally's cheeks and Kade's wolf growled. It didn't like their mate's tears.

"I missed you too."

The women plopped down on the couch next to him, and Kade managed to refrain from dragging his mate back into his lap. He'd promised to give her space, as tough as that was.

"So now it's my turn to get some answers," Lucy said, her voice full of excitement. "How in the world did you keep this secret from me for so long? Or has it not been 'so long'?"

She shot Kade a curious glance, but Ally shook her head. "He had nothing to do with it."

Ally's scent grew increasingly agitated, and he knew she didn't want to discuss her past. Not yet. He reached over and clasped her hand. She squeezed back, warming his heart. If Lucy noticed her friend's discomfort, it certainly didn't stop her.

"So, are you natural born like Mason and his brothers?"

Pause.

"No."

"How long have you been a wolf?"

Pause.

"Awhile."

"Does Pepper have a pack I don't know about?"

Pause.

"I don't…" Ally shook her head. "No."

"Then where's your pack? You have one, don't you?"

Pause, and this time her grip tightened.

"No." The word came out as a low rasp.

Kade leaned toward Ally and murmured, "You do now."

Lucy grew frustrated with Ally's short answers. "Come on, Ally. You've kept me in the dark this long—"

"So, a little longer won't hurt," Kade interrupted, pulling Ally upright as he stood. As much as he wanted the same answers as Lucy, it was obvious Ally wasn't up to revealing anything more. Not that night. "It's been a long day and I think we all need a good night's sleep."

Ally graced him with the loveliest smile of gratitude and his heart nearly burst. He would do anything for her, even cross the Alpha Mate, if it helped ease her nerves.

"Fine," Lucy grumped and stood. "We have guest rooms ready for both of you. Grandma, you'll be in a room just down the hall. Ally, you'll be upstairs—"

"Actually," Kade cut in, drawing Ally back against his chest. "Ally wants to stay with me."

Mason, Tessa, and Lucy all looked skeptical, but he didn't care. After everything she'd been through, he didn't want Ally to be alone in a strange house without anyone to protect her. Only Ally mattered now. No one else.

Ally turned her intense gaze up to meet his, her voice so soft he nearly missed what she said. "I do?"

"You do." Kade gave her a brisk nod, meeting her gaze with the same intensity. Ally still seemed unsure, the scent of her anxiety slowly drifting toward him, and he stepped into her space. He cupped her cheek, meeting her uneasy stare for a moment before leaning down and pressing his forehead to hers. "Come home with me, Ally. Let me be the one who stands between you and everything you fear."

She hesitated a moment and Kade held his breath, waiting for her decision. If she wanted to stay in the pack house, he'd let her. He'd also shift and patrol the area around the house.

"Ally?" Lucy spoke up once more and his mate pulled away. His wolf whined, not liking this new distance, but when her answer came, the beast calmed.

"I want to stay with Kade."

CHAPTER ELEVEN

Ally expected to be nervous about going home with Kade. Wary of him and his expectations, but she was simply... calm. Her wolf almost purred in her mind, the animal at peace knowing he was near. And would be near as she slept.

Kade held the front door open for her as he hustled her onto the porch. She gave Lucy a small wave and nod when her best friend said they'd see each other in the morning.

Mason stepped forward then, one of the largest werewolves she'd ever met, to speak to his brother, and she scuttled back a step. And then another. She lingered right at the edge of the first porch step. That still wasn't enough space for her unsettled inner wolf, her animal pacing and whimpering with the Alpha's nearness.

She decided waiting by the SUV was a better idea. She

silently traveled down the porch steps until her shoes sank into the moist grass. She even made it across the yard and all the way to Kade's car before she was stopped.

A large, strong hand landed on her shoulder—the grip firm but gentle—and spun her around. Even at that slight touch, a new surge of tingles rolled down her spine. She peered up at Kade with wide eyes and hoped the night hid the renewed blush on her cheeks.

"No need to take the SUV," Kade murmured and then waved his hand toward the right side of the pack house, "My place is here along the path."

Ally peered into the darkness, the shadows so deep she saw nothing beyond the midnight edges, and a bolt of fear pierced her heart. "It's so dark."

He smiled and pulled her into a gentle hug, those strong arms enveloping her. She sighed and turned her head, resting her cheek on his chest. She took comfort in his strength and the steady beat of his heart. Kade wasn't worried about a late night walk, so she shouldn't worry either. "I'll be right here. Always."

Ally drew in a deep breath with the hope that his musky scent would bring her comfort. Instead, all it did was make her tingle more. Those delicious sensations slid through her, nipples hardened and core aching to be touched.

Kade released her to snare her over-stuffed duffel, and her

wolf howled at the absence of his touch. If the beast had its way, she would have told him to leave the bag. That would let them slip under the sheets that much sooner.

Which hadn't sounded like a good idea until she'd heard Kade's whispered words and promises to protect her from her nightmares. Now, though... Her human half wasn't putting up much of a fight over sharing a bed with the big, bad, wolf.

"Ready?" Kade's deep voice broke through her thoughts.

Slinging the bag over his shoulder, he grabbed Ally's hand as if it was the most natural thing in the world. She allowed her fingers to curve around his calloused palm as they rounded the pack house and stepped onto the small path beyond. The night sky was inky black, and fluffy clouds covered the nearly full moon.

"The path is a little bumpy, so watch your step." He looked down at her, eyes reflecting the little light around them. "It might be easier to shift and take advantage of our wolves' vision."

"Uh, no." She shook her head, long ponytail brushing the base of her neck.

The last thing she wanted to do was set her wolf free. It had naughty fantasies of racing through the forest with Kade's beast. Of playing a game of chase and letting herself get caught by the tempting male. And once her wolf had its fill of the tempting shifter, it'd allow her to shift back, leaving her utterly naked. Kade would be nude as well and that... was just too much temptation for a gal to handle.

So, she let her decision stand. For now, there would be no shifting or naked playtimes featuring Ally and Kade. None.

A few minutes later, Kade strode up a walkway to the door of a smaller cabin. He nudged the door open and she followed him into the pure blackness. Details were lost to the lack of light, but she sensed this home was smaller than the pack house but still a nice, comfortable size. Any other clues about her home for the night would have to wait until the sun rose.

"It's not much, but it's home." A slight jitter underlaid those words, revealing his nervousness.

Kade flipped on the lights, illuminating a rustic bachelor pad. Just like the pack house, the place was decorated with hand-built log furniture, but unlike the immaculate pack house, Kade's looked as if a tornado had touched down in the middle of the living room.

"Shit!" He yanked a pair of boxer briefs off the back of the couch and held them behind his back, giving her a pleading look. "Pretend you don't see any of this. Give me one second."

The poor guy scuttled around the living room, grabbing dirty plates, grease-stained pizza boxes, and various articles of clothing off every surface. It barely made a dent in the mess, but at least he tried. He tossed all the clothes behind a chair tucked in a corner, dumped the dirty dishes into an already overflowing sink, and stuffed the pizza boxes into the oven.

Apparently the "if I can't see it, it doesn't exist" rule was in full effect.

She never would have believed such a self-assured guy like Kade could be nervous. It was actually pretty cute. Yes, his confidence was hot and drew her in, but this other side of him made Kade seem real. Made him a normal person and not some powerful, all-knowing, deadly werewolf.

"I, uh… I can give you a tour? As you can see, I wasn't expecting company when I went to collect Tessa. My place is normally… cleaner."

Ally didn't even have to draw in his scent to know he was lying about his cleaning habits. Maybe it wasn't ever *this* bad, but she had a feeling he was a bit of a slob. Yet she didn't care. She'd never felt so safe and protected in her life so if she had to deal with errant laundry and the Leaning Tower of Pizza-stained dishes, she would.

"It's beautiful, Kade." Sure, the lingering mess was like a layer of dust on furniture, but she could still sense its beauty.

She wandered from the living room to the kitchen. The counters were bare, not a single appliance, save a microwave. A slew of take-out menus were stuck to the fridge door with magnets.

"You don't have to lie." Kade scrubbed a hand over the back of his neck. "I know it's a little... homespun. My parents were dedicated to living with the land, so all the houses were built with as many locally sourced materials as possible."

That stopped her, and she furrowed her brow. "You built this house?"

"We all did. The pack comes together to help each other when the time comes. Sort of like a barn raising."

"Seriously?" She looked around the home again, looking for those handmade touches. For the bits and pieces that announced the home had been built with love by the pack. "I couldn't make a birdhouse and the pack..."

"Sure, you could," Kade insisted. "I'll teach you." When she tried to cover a yawn, he smiled. "But it might have to wait because right now, I think it's time for bed."

Until he said the words, she'd refused to acknowledge her exhaustion. She ignored the way sleep called to her and the pull of tiredness on her slumped shoulders. He led her down a short hallway and paused to identify the three closed doors. Starting on the right, he moved counter-clockwise, "Bathroom." Then the second door. "Guestroom. If you want it."

Ally stared up at him, utterly speechless. Of course, she wanted it...didn't she? Standing so close to him, feeling heat roil off his body like waves off a desert highway, smelling—it all made her head spin and her heart thunder.

Tension built between them, a sense of anticipation tempered with the lightest touch of anxiety teasing her nerves. He finally lifted a hand and jerked a thumb to the door behind him. "My room."

His soft gaze searched her face, somehow turning her on and breaking her heart at the same time. "Ally, I know you don't want to hear this, but the thought of being separated from you... When I'm not near you, it feels as if a limb is missing. As if part of mc has disappeared. Can you honestly tell me you don't feel the same?"

She opened her mouth to deny the charges, then snapped it closed again. For all he'd done for her—all he'd promised to do—she couldn't lie to him. Of *course,* she felt it. She never would have imagined it possible, but it was true no matter how many denials she voiced. The wolf's desire for him always turned her into a liar.

And that was the problem. The connection between the werewolf halves of them was nearly overpowering, but her wolf was only half of who she was. Her human side remained as confused as ever.

For years after her experience in Brian's pack, she'd assumed they all worked the same way. It was why she never sought out another and why she suppressed her animal's natural instincts. After her escape, she'd vowed to never subject herself to that kind of pain again. In reality, she'd simply traded one kind of pain for another —loneliness.

Now Kade stood before her, offering her so much. Not only a mate who really spun her cookies, but also a pack that didn't treat its members like servants—or worse. Safety. Love. Being surrounded by good people who would accept her as one of their own.

Everything she'd seen indicated that her assumption had been wrong—every pack *was not* like Brian's. Lucy had been happy and smiling. The pack house hadn't been caked in dirt and half destroyed by the latest gathering. One that'd ended in bloodshed and violence. True, she'd only been on pack lands for a few hours, so she couldn't be sure of anything, but... But after days in Kade's company, she felt like she could be sure of *him*. Sure, that he wouldn't allow her to come to harm—physically, anyway. As for her heart... she'd protect it from him as much as possible.

"Ally?"

Kade's gentle urging brought her gaze up to meet his. No, she couldn't deny her feelings for him, but she couldn't allow herself to succumb to them either. Not tonight.

"I—" Her voice caught in her throat, her wolf trying to

stop her from speaking. Clearing her throat, she tried again. "I think it's best if I stay in the guest room tonight."

Inside, her animal whined at the lack of gratification, but Ally wasn't in the mood to listen. She'd never let her beast rule her life in the past and she wasn't about to start now.

Bitter disappointment wafted through the narrow hallway. But she knew he wouldn't pressure her to change her mind. He might not be happy, but so far, she'd come to recognize that he was intent on making *her* happy.

So, when he nodded sadly and pulled her into his arms, she sank into the warm strength of his embrace, taking the comfort it offered. Within moments, the hallway filled with a different aroma, this one Kade's distinctive woodsy, smoky scent, with a healthy splash of spicy lust.

Her wolf growled, its desires clear—*do something. Don't just stand there.* Her skin flushed, and nipples tightened to hard nubs pressed against his firm chest.

Maybe it wasn't her wolf. In that moment, her halves seemed to blur and merge, their desires in sync. Without thinking about what she was doing, Ally tipped her head back to meet Kade's intense stare. No avarice, no deception, no evil intentions. All she saw was caring. Perhaps something that edged beyond caring and into the deeper waters of love.

Ally placed her hands on his biceps, slid them up his arms and across his shoulders to twine around his neck.

Fingers sinking into his hair, she urged him to bend down while she pressed to her tip-toes. Their lips met in a soft, sweet kiss. One she felt all the way to her toes. It was meant to be a small sign of appreciation. To thank him for his protection and understanding. For bringing her to this place she never imagined could exist. For making her feel safer than she had in years.

That was all it was meant to be.

The moment her lips touched his, all good intentions vanished in a rolling wave of desire. Her arousal mingled with the scent of his own, deep, dark longing and she drew those delicious flavors into her lungs. His tongue swept into her mouth while his hands found her hips, his hold urging her to turn and shuffle backward. Her back pressed against the guestroom door while his chest brushed against her sensitive breasts.

Her breath came in quick, needy pants, soft moans interspersed as he delved deeper and aroused her further. His hardness was firm against her hip, evidence of his need drawing a deep moan from the back of her throat. Kade reached around her, burying one hand in her hair while the other curled to squeeze her ass. Grip firm, he pulled her to him that much harder, his length pulsing against her hip, and her pussy clenched in response. She *ached*. For him. For more. For everything.

God, he felt good. Worse, he felt *right*. Like the missing piece of a puzzle she'd fought to solve her entire adult life.

He crowded closer, his chest like a brick wall against her soft breasts and her nipples straining against him. She sucked gently on the tip of his tongue, as much to silence her whimpering as to take in more of his taste.

Madness. Total insanity, and yet she tightened her arms and grinded against that thick bulge. Tremors radiated through her, pressure building low in her belly as he nipped sharply at her bottom lip.

His mouth was magic, his scent more intoxicating than the finest wine. She ought to break away. But the idea of chucking all of her carefully laid plans and following him into his bedroom seemed just as appealing. *More* appealing. She wanted him more than anything she'd ever wanted in her life. Needed him to fling her onto the bed and have his way with her. Needed to feel him hard and thick and deep inside her.

In spite of her wolf's most desperate efforts to distract her, a spark of sanity still glowed somewhere deep within her. That spark grew to an ember, then caught fire in her mind. It was all too much, too confusing. She'd spent so many years believing one thing, only to discover it may have never been true in the first place. It felt as if her brain was short-circuiting, and she needed space and time to let it all sink in. With a Herculean effort, Ally managed to push him back, panting as she looked into his hungry and confused eyes.

"I'm sorry... I..." she panted, not knowing what else to say.

Breaking off their kiss had probably done all the talking for her.

"What you want, when you want, and how you want, Ally." His voice came out as a hoarse rasp, his own wolf's growl in every syllable. She watched him fight his inner beast for control and win. "And no matter what, it's at your own pace."

There was no missing the desperate need etched into every line of his body, but she sensed the determination in his words. He ached for her, but he was taking a step back, giving her what she asked for without her having to say the words.

Standing on her tiptoes, she gave him a chaste peck on the cheek. His eyes fell closed and he leaned into her until she pulled away again. Turning the door knob behind her, she slowly backed into the guest room.

"Good night, Kade."

His heavy gaze stayed on her until the door shut him out. Pressing her forehead to the frame, she listened as his bedroom door opened and snicked closed quietly. Jelly had replaced her knees and her entire body shuddered as she managed to collapse on the bed instead of the floor.

"What have I done?" she whispered to the ceiling.

Now that she'd had a taste of Kade Blackwood, she couldn't imagine her life without him.

CHAPTER TWELVE

It'd taken Kade a good hour to pass out after the kiss he shared with Ally. Even then, his dreams had been filled with tempting images of his mate sprawled across his bed, no clothing in sight. He'd just trailed a line of kisses down her tummy and his lips teased the apex between her thighs when he was jerked awake by blaring sirens and flashing lights.

He leapt from the bed, fangs descended and fur covering his spine by the time his feet hit the floor. He strode from the room, finding a wide-eyed Ally standing in the hall wrapped in a comforter. Her gaze frantically swept the area, searching for the threat that triggered his alarm system. She spun his way, and to her credit, didn't so much as twitch when she saw his half-shifted state—or his nudity.

In the flashing of the lights, she looked so pale and small. His instincts were to gather her in his arms and comfort her, tell her everything was fine. But he needed to make sure everything was fine first.

"Stay here," he growled, before setting off to search the house.

The windows and doors were still secured, and he didn't catch any unusual scents in his home, but something had tried to breach his system. So, whoever it was hadn't gotten into the house—invaded his territory.

Probably just that dim-witted raccoon that liked to crawl around his window sills, not knowing that its presence sent his wolf into fits of slavering, murderous rage. Or maybe it was the smartest raccoon in the world and knew exactly what it was doing.

He punched a code into the alarm box by the door to turn off the blaring and flashing, then threw open the front door, ready to pounce… on nothing. The chirp of crickets and flavors of damp grass greeted him. Stepping onto the porch and closing the door behind him, he breathed in deeply, taking advantage of his wolf's senses even as he remained mostly human.

Deer. An owl. Red cedar. And… something *else*. Something that made his stomach churn and his blood pound in his temple.

The stench drifted on the wind—a condemned house, a

pile of garbage, dead things. The wolf that carried the foul odor of decay was not part of the Blackwood pack, but he wasn't an unknown. The fog of sleep still clouding his mind, it took a moment for Kade to recall where he'd encountered that aroma before.

The mystery wolf from Pepper.

Except this was fresher and the disgusting taint infinitely stronger. He followed the trail, more fur rippling across his body as he carefully padded across the yard—searching for evidence of an intruder. He froze in place when he found it. Kade stopped and stared at the unusual print among the scattered leaves and fallen twigs. Bold as day, even in the dark, lay a footprint. A *human* footprint. Not wolf, as he would have anticipated.

The problem was that the indentation was right in front of Ally's window.

The sight of that print transformed his anger into utter fury. Fury at the thought that some strange wolf invaded his territory—Blackwood territory—and watched his mate as she slept. The wolf asked for its freedom and he granted the request with ease. He gave it full reign and shifted between one heartbeat and the next.

Sniffing around the footprint and up the siding, he found deep gouges in the shape of claw marks on either side of the windows.

The creature had been half-shifted as he watched Ally. No

wolf left such destructive marks if they were intent on sitting down for a cordial afternoon tea. This was evidence of anger—rage—and riding the edge of control. Whoever this asshole was, he had nothing but ill intent toward Kade's mate.

Poor bastard just signed his own death warrant.

Kade snarled and spun in place, nose lowered as he followed the scent trail. His speed increased with every stride until he sprinted toward the tree line. His claws sought purchase in the damp earth and his ears were attuned to every sound that echoed through the night. The intruder had been clever—zigzagging through the forest as he'd made his escape—but it wasn't enough to throw Kade off his trail. Not when Ally's safety was at risk.

Silence surrounded him as he raced across the leaf-strewn floor. Every living creature sensing a ferocious and extremely pissed off predator in their midst. His massive paws kicked up chunks of dirt with every bound. Growls and snarls sent critters scampering away in the dark. Kade ignored them and kept his focus on the pungent intruder. The scent grew stronger and stronger the further he ran, until Kade sensed he was *this* close to capturing him. He still couldn't hear his prey, but the wolf had to be up ahead somewhere.

He put on more speed, focused on driving his prey to

ground and feel the male's throat between his jaws. That intense focus nearly cost him his life. He finally took a moment to check out his surroundings and realized where he was—right at the border of pack lands. More importantly, close to the river that formed that border.

He skidded and scrambled to a stop just as the sheer drop into the raging waters came into sight. He dug his claws into damp earth, searching for something to cling to as he slid the last few feet nearer to that edge. His forward movement stopped, and he remained poised in place for a moment before retreating and leaving the sticky mud behind. He sniffed along the water's edge, searching for that stranger's scent once more. Except it simply... stopped on the shore and vanished into nothingness.

Kade paced across the barren shore, peering into the darkness on the opposite side. He sought any hint of a presence—movement or a flash of amber eyes—but found nothing. That shitstain was over there somewhere but was too cowardly to confront him.

Which left Kade with a choice: wander the woods all night searching for the wolf, leaving Ally unguarded and vulnerable, or haul ass back to the house and protect her should the intruder try again. Fuck, why did he even bother asking himself the question. It wasn't a choice at all. Every cell in his body screamed for him to go to his mate's side and keep her safe.

Come first light, he'd speak with his brothers and make a plan of action. Bulk up defenses and put the sentries on alert. Send out their best trackers to investigate that section of their territory and hunt for clues. It would be good if Kade helped, but he refused to let Ally out of his sight until they found the strange smelling wolf.

Kade whirled and sprinted back to the house as fast as he could, finding Ally exactly where he'd left her. Except now she sat huddled in a corner, comforter tucked over her head and body trembling. The scent of her fear burned his tongue, her terror making his beast growl and snarl. It wasn't until she peeked from beneath the fabric and met his stare with terror-filled eyes that he realized his mistake.

Shit!

She'd already been skittish with the alarm and then he'd turned into a growling, dominant wolf. If he had managed to cling to some sense of calm, she wouldn't have panicked.

With a sigh, Kade closed his eyes and beckoned his wolf to return to its cage. It resisted at first, convinced it could do a better job at protecting than the human half, but he was persistent. He couldn't pull his mate close and comfort her without arms and hands. That one fact was enough for the animal. It gradually withdrew, and his fur receded, body reshaping to his human form.

Smiling was the last thing on his mind, but he'd try anything to calm her. And it worked... a little. She peeked past his shoulder, probably to confirm he hadn't been followed, and her shaking eased.

He motioned to the blanket. "Mind sharing?" He glanced down his body and waved a hand at himself. "It's a little chilly."

That earned him a flicker of a smile and the blanket itself. He wrapped it around his waist, then pulled her into him, loving the way they fit together.

After a long moment, she asked, "What happened?"

Telling the truth might scare her even more, but keeping secrets was unthinkable. Mates didn't hide anything from each other.

"Someone was prowling around the house." He smoothed her hair as he spoke, enjoying the feel of her silken tresses against his palm. "That's why we have alarms, though. I'm sure—"

"Where?" Ally demanded.

"What do you mean?"

"*Where* were they prowling? The kitchen, the front door, where?"

Kade braced himself. "Your room."

The trembles that had almost subsided returned with a

vengeance and her voice was hardly a whisper when she spoke. "Only my room?"

"It appears that way, but I chased him to the edge of our lands. Unfortunately, he crossed the river and I lost his scent."

"S-so…he's still out there?" Her voice—and body —trembled.

He squeezed her tighter. "I'm afraid so, but only a moron would try again tonight after all that commotion. No way he's returning, Ally. And if he does…"

The threat hung there, unspoken but completely understood.

"Can I stay with you tonight?" she whispered, her eyes pleading.

In spite of everything that happened, his cock went rigid in an instant. The last thing she'd want in her current state was to make love, but he couldn't help the way his body reacted to her.

Rather than allow the moment to turn awkward, he grinned down at her and comically waggled his eyebrows. "It would be my pleasure!"

The tentative smile from before grew into a small laugh. She slapped his chest lightly and color returned to her face, which gave him no small measure of relief.

"Sleep only, mister. No funny business."

He kicked at an imaginary dust bunny and pouted like a toddler. "Aw shucks."

She rested her head on his chest and they stood that way for a moment, simply holding one another, before she spoke again.

"I'm just too afraid to sleep alone," she softly confessed.

"I know," he murmured into her hair, closing his eyes and taking a deep breath.

"I do feel... *something* for you. I just... I'm just not ready to explore that right now."

Either his heart was about to burst or shrivel, he wasn't sure which. She'd just admitted she had feelings for him, which was a *major* score on his part, but she was still resisting their bond. Frustrating as hell, but it didn't matter. He'd do anything for her, even sleep by her side with one foot on the floor, if that was what she wanted.

He kissed the top of her head and released her. "I understand. You'll tell me when you're ready. We'll go at your pace. If you want to just sleep, that's all we'll do. If you want more..."

He waggled his eyebrows again and led her by the hand to his big king bed. She wore pretty pink silky pajamas that Kade wanted to tear off her body. Once they were both under the covers, he pulled her close into him, until her ass snuggled up against his still stiff cock.

"Hey, I said I just wanted to sleep," she teased.

"I know," he said with a happy sigh. "But I'll be damned if I fall asleep without you in my arms."

CHAPTER THIRTEEN

ALLY CHEWED ON A RAGGED THUMBNAIL, ATTENTION wholly focused on the entire Blackwood pack milling around in the pack house yard. The thick clouds that had blacked out the full moon mere days ago were nowhere in sight, allowing the area to be bathed in an ethereal glow. The mood of the other wolves was happy and excited, some of them already shifted and racing around the yard in their wolf forms.

Carefree. Joyful. But their overwhelming happiness wasn't enough to soothe the ragged edge of her anxiety. She hadn't been around so many werewolves in her life and this…

An arm flopped across her shoulders, followed by someone's head tipped to rest against hers. The familiar touch, familiar scent, soothed her inner wolf. *Lucy.*

"I'm so glad you decided to join us on our run."

"Yeah, um, me too." Mostly. Partly. Not at all.

Lucy laughed and squeezed Ally's shoulder. "Don't sound so excited, Al. Haven't you ever been on a pack run?"

She shrugged, still not ready to discuss her past with anyone, even her best friend.

"Well, you're going to love it. It's a monthly tradition. No speeches, no ceremonies. It's just a fun way for the pack to strengthen its bond and enjoy the call of the moon."

It made sense. She'd felt the pull of the moon many times over the years, but never so strongly. In fact, ever since Kade had come into her life, everything about being a werewolf had intensified. Including her wolf's delight in finally being able to run free. After years of suppressing the craving to feel dirt under her paws and wind in her fur, the beast practically howled with joy. And sharing that experience with a group of people who seemed to *not* want to kill her sounded pretty nice. If it weren't for one, small thing...

"Why is everyone undressing?"

"Are you kidding?" Lucy gave her an incredulous look. "We'd shred our clothes if we shift without getting naked. I love shopping as much as you do, Ally, but that's a little too wasteful. Plus, I like this shirt. Oh, Mason's calling me. See you in the woods!"

Lucy ran off toward the Alpha, tugging her shirt off and tossing it aside as she went. She wasn't the only one to leave piles of clothing around. No one else hesitated to show off what their mama gave them. Except Ally. The very idea of exposing herself made her skin itch, hives threatening to make an appearance. The feeling intensified when she imagined Kade's gaze on her. Not that he posed a threat, but some reactions were simply instinctual after what she'd experienced.

True to his word, in the two nights since Brian had set off the alarm, Kade had done nothing more than spoon her as they fell asleep. With his warm, strong arms wrapped tight around her—and the knowledge that Blackwood sentries were patrolling the perimeter—she'd never slept more soundly.

Other sentries kept an eye on her throughout the day as well, but far from feeling smothered, Ally was relieved by that extra show of protection. Brian was out there, biding his time, but the Blackwood pack stood together to protect her—a stranger—from an unknown threat. She'd never experienced this feeling of peace in the past and that sensation merely doubled when Kade was at her side.

The only hiccup in her life at the moment was Kade and the time they spent together at night. Whenever they were snuggled up in bed, his larger body curling around hers, all she wanted was to roll over and start something she didn't want to stop. Ever. He'd been a perfect gentleman, and there were no wandering hands or roving lips. Despite his belief that they were mates, he kept it strictly PG. Which merely infuriated and frustrated her wolf, because the beast wanted to jump to a XXX rating.

Okay, maybe it wasn't just her wolf who felt hot and bothered and desperate for the big wolf's bod.

The tender, chaste approach was what she'd needed when they met, but now... Now she'd spent time with him, gotten to know him alone as well as watched him interact with the pack, and found herself aching for more. What they'd had was no longer enough. She wasn't sure *what* she craved, but she knew exactly *who* she desired.

And glancing around the area, she gritted her teeth when she realized Kade was nowhere to be seen.

Something tugged at the back of her shirt, the pull gentle but insistent. Spinning in place she peered down at little Charlie while he stared at her, his head cocked to the side. If he'd been a pup, she had no doubt his ears would have been perked up in an unasked question. Of course, he was human-shaped, so the questions came at her rapid-fire.

"Why do you still have your clothes on, Ally? Aren't you going on the run with everyone else? Do you want to help me take care of Ghost Kitty and her babies? Ooh, was that a bat? Cool!"

Since she'd arrived on Blackwood lands, she'd spent a little time with the boy, who had proudly told her he was "five and three-quarters." Then he'd launched into a story about how Ghost Kitty and all her kittens were his because he'd saved them from a burning porch, whatever that meant. Despite the kid's incessant chatter, he really was quite a charmer and she'd grown fond of the pup.

Ally wasn't sure which of his questions to answer first, so she started with the easiest. "Yes, that was a bat. No, I can't help you with the kitties because yes, I'm going on the run. Aren't you?"

The boy's lower lip pooched out so far Ally worried he might sprain it. "No."

"Why?" She tried not to snicker at his pouting.

"Mama says I'm too little, so I have to stay behind with Ida, Tessa and all the *babies*." He spat the last word as if it tasted like rotten meat.

"That'll be fun though, won't it?"

"Not as fun as running!" He rolled his shoulders back and stuck his nose up in the air. "Besides, I'm big now. I'm too old for a babysitter."

Ally had only briefly met Ida Abbot, the woman who managed the pack house, but Tessa was sure to show the kids a good time. "Hey, Lucy's grandma is a pretty fun lady."

He didn't look convinced.

Ally lowered to a crouch, putting herself at eye-level with Charlie. She tugged on his shirt and smiled at the young boy. "I'm sorry my first run with the Blackwood pack will be without my second favorite pack member."

Charlie's face split into a huge grin. "Bet I know who your first favorite is!"

He mimed a kissy face at her, then skipped away, singing at the top of his lungs. "Kade and Ally, sitting in a tree, K-I-S-S-I-N-G."

"I like the sound of that," a deep voice rumbled behind her, and she rose, turning to find Kade standing behind her, hands stuffed in the pockets of his low-slung jeans. Low-slung and loose so that his hands tugged the denim even lower. "Ready?"

Ally was ready for something.

She glanced around the yard once more, unable to suppress her newest rush of nerves. It'd been years since she'd been around so many wolves, but the mood here was so different than it had been back then. Their excitement was infectious, and she was almost ready to pound the ground alongside them. The rest of her wanted to run in the opposite direction as long and far as she could go.

Before she could bolt, Kade wrapped an arm around her shoulders and rubbed her arm. Her nerves instantly settled with the touch and her mind moved on to thinking about running through the forest by his side all night long.

Like everything in life, starting was the hardest part. It was doubly hard in this case because it meant stripping down.

In front of everyone.

Including Kade.

She wasn't ashamed of her body. She'd simply never been much of an exhibitionist.

As yet another pack member shimmied out of his pants, dick just swinging in the breeze, Ally blushed and hid her face in Kade's chest. She didn't think she'd ever be that free and easy when it came to undressing in a crowd.

A chuckle rumbled through Kade's chest and he tipped her chin up, forcing her to meet his gaze. "I had no idea you were such a prude. Let's take turns." He stepped back and whipped his white t-shirt over his head, giving Ally a full view of his sculpted abs. "See? No big deal. Now you."

Ally winced and glanced around to see if anyone watched them. Not a soul. Everyone else was too focused on preparing for the run themselves. She toyed with the top button of her shirt, and just as she was about to unfasten it, she sensed the presence of someone behind her.

A jolt of alarm poured adrenaline into her system and she whirled in place, half-expecting to find Brian glaring down at her. Instead, she found the youngest Blackwood brother, Gavin, nearby.

Just like everyone else, Gavin was only partially dressed. Barefoot and shirtless, his jeans already unzipped to reveal a light dusting of hair that grew denser the lower her eyes roamed. Thwarted by the rest of his jeans, she let her gaze skim up the ridges and bulges that made up his stomach and chest, until she reached his handsome gray eyes.

No doubt about it, Gavin Blackwood was just as gorgeous as his older brothers, but not in a way that tripped her trigger. He quirked a suggestive eyebrow at her then winked, and his lips curled up in a sensual smirk. She blushed and fidgeted, uneasy at being the subject of his attention. It felt... wrong. And kinda gross, to be honest. Aside from appreciating his beauty in a clinical way, Ally had zero interest in the youngest Blackwood. She definitely didn't want anyone looking at her with sex on the brain except Kade.

Without warning, Kade hoisted her over his shoulder, ass up and head down, and brushed past his laughing brother.

"What are you doing?" She didn't bother fighting him. She was far too busy enjoying the hardness of his muscles and the smoky heat of his scent as he carried her to the far side of the pack house.

"You were right." His voice was rough and gravelly with

emotion. "You shouldn't undress in front of the pack until you're more comfortable."

She nearly snorted. Nearly. He could lie all he wanted, but she scented the truth in the air. Every step sent up the strong, spicy scent of jealousy. One giggle led to two and by the time they rounded the corner and he placed her on her feet, she was laughing outright. Which earned her a scowl.

"What's so funny?"

This only made her laugh harder and she shook her head with disbelief. "You! You're jealous!"

He scoffed and sniffed and snorted, but he didn't deny her words.

"Admit it, you're jealous."

Kade gripped her hips, squeezing gently while he walked her backward until her back rested against the wall. He stooped, leaning down until his blazing eyes were level with her own.

"I'm jealous." He growled low, but the threatening sound didn't scare her the least bit. "I want you more than I want my next breath, Ally. I die a little every time I have to restrain myself from kissing you."

The smile fell from Ally's lips and her body responded to his words. Every nerve flickered to life, flames dancing over the endings. Mere inches separated them, his lips so very, very close, and she couldn't stop staring at Kade's mouth.

She licked her lips, unsure what to say. "I—"

"Ally, I'd never push you. I'd never do anything you didn't want. I know how to control myself, but I can't pretend it's easy."

Dragging her gaze from the lips she longed to kiss, she met his intense gaze. "Kade, I... I definitely have feelings for you, and I'm trying to figure out what they are. I've never felt anything like this in the eight years I've been a wolf."

Kade's eyes widened at her unintended admission and Ally kicked herself for letting such a revealing detail about her life slip out. She'd worked hard to build up her defenses, but just a few days around Kade Blackwood and they were gradually crumbling to dust.

In for a penny...

She swallowed past the knot of apprehension in her throat and opened up to him a little more. "And it scares the hell out of me."

CHAPTER FOURTEEN

Kade reeled, not only from Ally's confession, but also her nearness. He couldn't stop himself from pulling in as much of that sweet milk and honey aroma coming off her skin as he could. He fought the intoxicating effects of her flavors and struggled to focus. He couldn't allow himself to become distracted. Not when she'd just truly opened up to him for the first time.

"So, you were made, not born," he concluded gently.

Ally dropped her gaze and shrugged.

"How?" He kept his voice calm and low while his wolf raged in his mind. She'd been made. Probably painfully, violently.

She looked away and pressed her lips together. The window of opportunity to learn more of her was closing fast. He tried for an easier question.

"Where's your pack?"

She sniffed and finally met his gaze. "I've never had one. Not really."

Kade couldn't wrap his head around what she was telling him. She'd been born human, then turned into a werewolf, which meant she was bitten. Bitten with no mate and no pack. No protection. How was she even alive? He couldn't ask *that* yet, as much as he wanted to hear the answer. Besides, it was pretty obvious—she was strong as hell.

"If you never had a pack to learn from, you must not know much about your abilities."

"I suppose that's true, but I've picked up the basics along the way. I learned to control my wolf on my own. I learned I heal more quickly than... before. I learned to sniff out other wolves and keep my distance. I read some books on natural wolves, but I haven't found many credible texts on werewolves."

Try 'none', Kade thought ruefully, amazed by her strength and bravery.

"It must have been hell for you," he said, thumb stroking her hip.

"I discovered a few benefits. It's why I'm such a good dog walker. It's pretty easy to keep them all in line because I'm always the alpha of the pack." She flashed him a cheeky grin with that and his heart broke.

It was a strange 'bright side', but when you were surrounded by darkness, the faintest blip of light must seem as bright as the sun. Now that she was speaking more freely, he asked the question burning inside him.

"Eight years ago… You must have been fresh out of high school." He lowered his voice and softened his eyes, so she would know it was safe to confide in him. "What happened, Ally?"

A veil dropped over her eyes and she pulled herself from his embrace, moving just out of reach. She pretended it was, so she could peek around the corner at the rest of the pack, but he sensed her discomfort. Unable or unwilling to answer the question, he knew better than to press his mate. As frustrating as it was, he at least had another piece of the puzzle his mate presented. Kade leaned against the wall, his attention on Ally while he waited for her to quit pretending to be interested in the crowd.

"No wonder you don't recognize what we have."

She tensed and returned her attention to him, her brows pulled low over her narrowed eyes. "This again?"

He ignored the comment. "I thought you wanted to take your time, but you really don't understand, do you?" No answer, just lips pressed into a thin line to join her glare. "I'm talking about fated mates, Ally. I know humans don't have them, but werewolves do. We mate for life. When we discover our mate, we become whole. Our souls intertwine and connect us forever. Those feelings you're trying to deny? Trying to fight? You won't win because we're destined to be together. Just like Lucy and Mason."

Ally's eyes grew wide and a fresh red glow spread over her cheeks. "Now hold on—"

"I won't let you hide from the truth any longer," he said, pushing off the wall and grasping her shoulders. "I know how hard it must be for you to process, but you can't hide away this part of you much longer or you'll go feral."

"Feral?" She blinked up at him.

"Wolves who don't find their mates—or in your case, deny them—will eventually go feral. Basically, you'll go insane and start killing any and everything you can. Lucy's parents were killed by a feral wolf."

Ally gasped, and all color drained from her face.

"It's true. That wolf went feral for different reasons, but the end result was the same. I won't let that happen to you, Ally. The sooner you accept all there is to being a werewolf, the happier you'll be, I promise."

She clearly had her doubts, as evidenced by the deep furrow in her brow. "I don't know…"

"But I do," he countered. "I know you feel drawn to me in a way you can't explain. I know your wolf won't let you deny your feelings. It claws and howls to be set free, so we can finally be together. You're having trouble controlling your beast. You catch the slightest whiff of my scent and your wolf goes nuts. Touching me helps ease the desperate ache inside you, but it's not enough. Not nearly enough."

Throughout his little speech, Ally's eyes grew wider and wider. "How did you…?"

He traced her ruffled brow with his forefinger, reveling in the sparks of electricity that shot up his arm and straight to his heart. "Because it's exactly how I feel. It's how *all* fated mates feel."

Tears welled in her eyes as her head and her heart battled one another. Her confusion caused a physical pain inside him. "I wish I could believe you, but I just—"

He wrapped his arms around her trembling frame and pulled her into a deep hug. He rested his cheek atop her head and took comfort in the knowledge that she didn't pull away. "You'll trust me someday. Soon, I hope. For now, I need you to know that members of the Blackwood pack are honorable and kind. We aren't violent, unless it's to protect one of our own from outsiders. No one throws their dominance around just because they can. There is no belittling or attacking of weaker wolves." Ally tried to respond but her voice was so thin it broke. He gave her a squeeze, then released her. "What I really want to know right now is whether you still want to go on tonight's run."

Almost as if in answer to his question, a howl split the

night air. Mason calling the pack to shift and dive into the forest. His howl was answered by dozens more, and Kade's own wolf surged forward, ready to follow their Alpha. Ready to run off some of his pent-up frustration.

But only if he had Ally by his side. If she didn't want to go, he'd stay behind to make sure she was safe and secure, if not exactly happy.

Stepping back from him, she took a deep breath and her fingers went to the top button on her shirt. "Let's run."

CHAPTER FIFTEEN

THE EXCITEMENT IN KADE'S EYES WAS ECHOED IN ALLY'S heart. She normally kept her wolf on a tight leash, but now she could hardly wait to cede control to her inner animal. Let it out to race through the woods and enjoy the feel of the wind stroking her fur.

Kade's hands dropped to the fly of his jeans and instinct told her to look away, but her wolf growled a warning. It wanted to watch him strip. It wanted to witness his strength—the way his pecs flexed, and muscles bunched and moved as he undressed. He was, without a doubt, the sexiest man she'd ever seen. Only when his hands stopped moving did she look up at his face.

He wore a seductive smile which sent a flush of heat from her hairline and straight to her core. Human embarrassment forced her to finally turn away, but that couldn't stop her body's reaction—the deep ache—to the large male.

Fumbling with the buttons on her own shirt, Ally managed to shrug it off her shoulders. She peeked over her shoulder to see if he watched her—hoping he was—and got more than she bargained for. So much more!

Just as her eyes landed on Kade, his pants and boxers fell from his hips, giving her a full, unobstructed view of everything he had to offer. Her breath caught, and mouth went dry for a split-second. Then it flooded with saliva as her wolf begged her to drop to her knees and take him in her mouth. To feel his hardness stretch her eager lips. To suck and lick and moan until he weaved his fingers in her hair and groaned in bliss. To see if he tasted like he smelled—smoky cherry wood.

When his eyes dropped to her diamond-hard nipples, Ally fought not to let her mind wander further. She definitely wasn't going to think about his lips wrapping around one of those firm nubs and flicking it with his tongue. *Nope.*

Her fingers froze on the button of her shorts and her knees felt as if they might buckle at any moment. She couldn't figure out if she was literally weak in the knees, or if her body was overruling her mind and was trying to follow through on her fantasy of tasting Kade.

Horrified and exhilarated at the same time, Ally tore her attention away from the most gorgeous man in the known universe and stripped with a speed she didn't know she possessed. The moment the last piece of clothing hit the ground, she embraced her beast. She released her wolf and let the shift flow through her. Hurrying to complete her transformation before Kade got a chance to ogle the goodies for too long.

Her body twitched and everything about her seemed to *tug*. Fine arm hair sprouted into dense fur. Her face pulled into a long snout. Her bones compressed and adjusted until two legs became four. Her body turned into something lean and confident. Glancing down at her thick paws in the dirt, she panted with happiness. Her fur rippled along her spine with the immensely satisfying sense of release. Almost—but not quite—like a good orgasm.

Is there such a thing as a bad *orgasm?* she wondered as she scratched at the ground with glee. Her nails sank into the dirt, cool grass tickling her toes.

Movement caught her eye. Kade had shifted too, his dark fur almost glowing in the moonlight. His musky, woodsy scent was stronger now, or maybe it was simply the heightened senses of her wolf. Regardless of the reason, she snuffled the air in his direction, pulling in more of his scent.

He stepped closer, confident in his movements but cautious in his approach. Considering how her human half behaved, she couldn't blame him, but now that she was in her wolf form, she was eager to explore their bond.

He nuzzled her neck, and his aroma turned into a taste and asserted the truth. The magnetic pull she'd felt, her absolute *need* for him, was not a fleeting infatuation. He'd hadn't been lying or trying to trick her. She felt it all the way to her bones. It suffused her, taking over every cell and nerve ending. Kade was her mate and would be for as long as they both lived.

The realization slammed into her like a train. She'd spent her adult life in abject misery—some days far worse than others. The last few years had been the happiest she could recall, but compared to the joy welling up inside her at that moment... they'd been total garbage.

If she were on two legs instead of four, she might have been overwhelmed by the fierce emotions and break down into tears. As a wolf, she couldn't contain her excitement. She yipped and barked, jumping away from Kade before darting forward once more. Her animal wanted to play, wanted to run into the dark woods.

Chirping insects and hooting owls fell silent as they tore through the forest, the nearest apex predators. Having denied herself the pleasure of running in wolf form for so long, Ally drank in every last luminous detail. The sharp ridges of tree bark, cool dirt embedded between her toes, the smell of dozens of nearby animals she never would have scented as a human.

And, of course, the scent of Kade as he loped and dashed in the trees next to her. They playfully raced for the lead spot, back and forth, only occasionally catching sight or scent of their pack mates as they raced. Ally suspected the others instinctively knew to keep their distance from the new mates, including the omnipresent sentries. They were with the pack, and yet they might as well have been a million miles away.

They crashed through undergrowth, Ally still in the lead, when Kade nipped her left haunch. He made a series of yips that her wolf easily interpreted. She swerved to the right and delved through even denser brush, bushes and trees tugging on her fur. They burst out of the thickest shrubbery and into a large clearing.

A small lake glittered in the moonlight, surrounded by big flat rocks, perfect for lazy afternoon basking. The peaceful water beckoned her forward, and she padded to the shore, slaking her thirst with the cool water. She sought Kade in the darkness and found him standing a few feet behind her. He was no longer a fierce and powerful dark-furred wolf, but a fully formed man ready to claim his mate.

His muscles bulged, the moonlight accentuating the deep shadows of his body. His cock stood out thick and hard from his body, the head a rich purple from arousal. But what stole her concentration was his expression—as naked and vulnerable as the rest of him. He was a werewolf aching for his mate, a male in love asking his fated female to accept him.

This time it was Ally's heart that tugged, and without a moment's hesitation, her wolf pulled back. Her fur tickled as it retracted into her body and her muscles quivered as they shrank into a weaker form. Before she could take a full breath, she stood before her mate on two legs, completely exposed in a way she'd never dreamed possible.

Wordlessly, he held out a hand to her and she stepped forward, her hesitation in the past. She knew the truth now. Whatever had happened in the past, Kade was honorable, strong and caring. He was everything she might have hoped for in a mate. She'd be a fool to deny it any longer.

CHAPTER SIXTEEN

KADE HAD EXPECTED ALLY TO BACK AWAY FROM HIS outstretched hand, to remain hesitant and uneasy despite the look of desire in her expression. Though deep inside he'd hoped that the moment she shifted, any doubt about their bond would evaporate. As her cool, silken palm ghosted over his thick calluses, he still was unsure of her intention. She twined her fingers with his and he couldn't suppress the joy building within. They were both nude, wearing only moonlight, and his mate had come to him.

He held her at arm's length for a moment, drinking in her beauty. Long waves of mussed hair the color of chocolate cascaded over her shoulders, curling just before they reached the dusky peaks perched on ample breasts. Her waist curved in, then her hips flared, showcasing her perfect, trimmed patch of hair at the juncture of her thighs. His mouth watered at the thought of spreading those legs wide and lapping at her sweet pussy.

Kade finished his perusal and then pulled her into him, not stopping until her full breasts brushed his chest while his hard length nestled against the soft curve of her lower stomach. Wrapping his arms around her, he buried his nose in her hair and breathed her in—a heady mix of wolf and aroused woman.

Despite the way his fingers itched to cup her breasts, to clutch the rounded curve of her ass, to savor every inch of her body until he knew it by heart, he held himself in check. There would be time enough for all of that, and only when Ally was ready.

"Thank you for trusting me, Ally," he murmured into her hair, delighting in the goosebumps that crawled along her flesh in response. "And trusting the pack enough to run with us. Someday, I'll have your complete trust, and that's when you'll share what's troubling you."

Ally tipped her head back to look up at him, her expression earnest. "I—"

"Shhh." He pressed a finger lightly to her lips, entranced as it skimmed the supple surface. What would it feel like to press his mouth to hers? To feel those plump lips move in time with his own? Shaking himself, he continued. "Not tonight. Tonight's meant for fun, running, and maybe getting to know each other a little better. How does that sound?"

Ally's arms snaked around his waist and she smiled up at him. That glorious smile, her closeness, nearly made his heart burst.

"It sounds perfect."

Leading her to a smooth platform of rocks at water's edge, he helped her climb until they reached a level slab. Kade pulled Ally across his lap as he sat, the need to hold her overwhelming all thoughts. Even though he had no intention of pressing her into anything physical, he ached to have her close. The moment she felt his hard cock nudge her thigh, the sweet blush he'd come to know and love swept across her cheeks.

A low groan escaped his lips and Ally shot him a mocking glare. He just shrugged in response. He wouldn't apologize for craving her. "You're my mate. What do you expect?"

She couldn't hold the glare for long and finally rested her head one his shoulder with a deep, satisfied sigh. Their fingers remained entwined, and when she stroked the palm of his hand with the tip of her thumb, he nearly lost what little control remained. It was such a chaste, tender touch, and yet his dick throbbed as if she' stroked him from root to tip over and over again. His balls ached and a desperate wanting thrummed beneath his skin.

"Tell me more about this whole fated mate thing." She kept her voice low, but she wasn't hesitant in her curiosity anymore. Still, the tightness in her voice concerned him.

Maybe talking about mates would draw him back from the edge of release. "The fated mate bond is something that is recognized instantly and can never be broken."

"Like Samuel L?"

"Huh?"

She sighed and shook her head. "Samuel L. Jackson? In *Unbreakable?*"

"Speak English, woman," he said with a laugh.

"I did! You're clearly not a film buff."

He rolled his eyes. "I have better things to do with my time."

"Like what?"

"Like tickle you!"

He tickled her waist, drawing squeals of delight and extreme torture from her. A sentry appeared at the edge of the clearing, ready to pounce. After seeing they were simply playing, he backed into the foliage until he disappeared. Kade hated that they were there—he wanted to protect his mate all by himself—but was also grateful for their presence. Until Ally told him everything, he'd need all the help he could get.

"Seriously," he finally said, after the giggles had subsided. "Mating for wolves isn't a pact or a promise. It's destiny. Werewolves can sense their mate before they even see them."

"How?"

He cuddled her close again and looked over the sparkling water, the moon's reflection dancing on the trembling surface. He recalled the first time he'd caught her scent back in Pepper. Had it been only days ago?

"In our case, I caught your scent the second I opened the car door. I'd just parked on Front Street because I wanted to grab a coffee before heading over to Tessa's. The smell was faint, and the coffee shop nearly overpowered it, but somehow your natural scent made it through. I spent the better part of a week trying to track you down."

"Stalker much?" she teased.

Kade grimaced. "Yeah, I guess that doesn't sound good, but I knew. I knew you were my mate the instant I caught your scent."

She lifted an arm and sniffed her armpit. "Maybe I should switch deodorants."

"Wouldn't make a difference," he shook his head and chuckled at her antics. "You know as well as anyone that perfumes can't mask a wolf's natural scent."

A shadow flitted across her features, disappearing as

quickly as it'd come to life, and she smiled. "There's just so much I don't know about our kind. About *me*, if you really think about it hard."

"Ask me anything."

Ally snorted. "You're gonna regret that after I get started. How do packs work? How does the Blackwood pack work?"

Her phrasing begged an obvious question—how could she *not* know how a pack was run? But, he'd promised to answer questions, not ask them.

"A wolf's position in a pack is determined by a few factors. Mostly their strength, scent or ability to meet another wolf's gaze without looking away. Heredity plays a part in all of those characteristics, so the title of Alpha often passes to the oldest son. In the Blackwood pack, the Alpha, Beta and Enforcer—Mason, me and Gavin, respectively—are the strongest, and we're the sons of the previous Alpha."

"Your father was Alpha? Did he quit or…"

Kade's heart clenched inside his chest, the grief still fresh even after years. "He passed away a few years ago. Our mother died when we were all young."

Sadness clouded Ally's beautiful face, but not pity. The look she gave him was empathetic, as if she'd suffered much loss in her life as well.

"I'm sorry, Kade."

He kissed the tip of her nose and held her closer still. "Thanks."

"So, you guys must rule with iron fists, right? Sons of the alpha and all of you in control..." she finally said, her tone wary.

"What?" He furrowed his brow and shook his head. "No. We instill discipline in the pack, especially with our sentries. They're the werewolf version of police, so they're highly skilled in combat. That training can be tough and often violent, but the average pack member goes about their lives. They just occasionally turn into a wolf now and again."

"What about when someone breaks a rule? They get punished, right?"

Kade didn't like that she seemed to think the worst of his pack, but it made him wonder once again what kind of life she'd lived as a wolf.

"Sometimes," he admitted, "but it depends on what happened. If one of our pack goes rogue, it's our duty to take him down. Our primary goal is the protection of the pack."

"Rogue, as in killing or transforming humans against their will?"

"That's oddly specific." He eyed her, his heartbeat racing

while unease knotted his stomach. Had she been changed... "But the answer is yes. We've had to put down more than one rogue wolf. In fact, Mason was on the verge of going feral when he and Lucy found each other. It would have been Gavin's and my duty to put him down if that had happened."

"Oh my God, that's horrible!"

It would have felt horrible, but it was their way. "Thank goodness we didn't have to, but we were prepared for that eventuality. The three of us talked about it at length, and Mason instructed us in no uncertain terms to do it as soon as he tipped over the edge of sanity. His focus is on the pack, not himself, which is how it is in every healthy pack. Even if we don't always like each other, we all love and protect each other."

Ally sighed and sank into him, bonelessly relaxing in his embrace. "It's like a big family."

"Exactly." He wanted to remind her that she was all but a member of their family now but didn't want to spook her. "What else do you want to know?"

"There's something I've always wondered... No, never mind. It's too embarrassing."

He jostled her. "C'mon, lay it on me."

"Okay, but no laughing. Promise?"

"Scout's honor."

"I know we're not exactly like natural wolves or dogs, but we obviously *are* like them in some respects. I haven't spent a lot of time around other wolves so…"

"Spit it out, woman!"

Ally laughed, the sound tinkling across the open expanse. "Okay, okay. Do werewolves sniff each other's' butts when they meet?"

Kade tried really hard not to laugh, but he couldn't stop his body from shaking. Finally, it bubbled up out of him into a snort, followed by a bout of chuckles that left him breathless. He was vaguely aware of Ally twisting in his arms and glaring up at him, but it was just too funny.

"Hey, you promised!" She poked him in the chest.

Kade got control of himself and pulled her back into a snuggling position. "Sorry, I couldn't help it. You're just so cute." He cleared his throat. "On occasion, when meeting new wolves from a different pack *in wolf form*, we might have a sniff or two. But we don't wander around in human form sticking our noses up other people's asses. Not literally, anyway."

It was her turn to laugh. "What about collars?"

"Ooh, kinky!" His cock, which had relaxed during their talk, sprang back to life against her leg.

"No, perv!" she said, lightly slapping his bicep. "I mean, you know, like dog collars. For control."

"No, we don't wear or force anyone to wear collars. Of course, what they do behind closed doors is no one's business."

Ally sighed and chuckled, then relaxed into him once more. He kissed her cheek, then pressed his against hers as they watched the starlight sparkling on the water like a million diamonds. Every so often, a Blackwood wolf would dart up to the far side of the lake and slake its thirst before bounding back into the forest. Some teenage wolves performed a playful mock battle, practicing their fighting skills, until one got nipped just a little too hard and yelped before trotting off toward the pack house. He saw no signs of the sentries, but he knew they were there, keeping everyone safe.

Contentment settled over him like a cozy wool blanket on a chilly night. He'd never imagined his heart could feel so full of love. He had his mate, snuggled in his arms, and his pack surrounded him. There was nothing in the world he wouldn't do for a single one of them.

CHAPTER SEVENTEEN

ALLY AND KADE SPRINTED THROUGH THE FOREST, YIPS AND snarls and howls echoing around them. Ally growled in mock anger when Kade bumped into her, knocking her off her stride and taking the lead in their little race. She wasn't normally competitive, but this was just too much fun for her to resist.

Running with an entire wolf pack had seemed so intimidating in the past. Terrifying, really. Yet Ally couldn't remember a more pleasurable night since she'd been turned. She didn't want it to end, but the stars in the moon hung low in the western sky. Dawn drew near, and they all had human things to do tomorrow. Things she could barely wait to experience.

Digging deep inside for an extra boost of speed, Ally gained on Kade, even though he was so much bigger. With a mighty lunge, she managed to get a mouthful of his tail fur and jerked her head for all she was worth. Kade barked, then tumbled while Ally took the lead once again.

All's fair, she thought with a snicker. *Even when he's your mate.*

The night had been amazing, but the time they'd spent on the rocks by the lake had been pure magic. They'd talked and watched the others frolicking, all the while Kade no doubt thinking she still wasn't sure about their connection. That doubt had disappeared the moment she'd released her wolf, but she still needed time to process it all.

Kade's paws tore through the twigs and leaves behind her, so Ally urged her wolf to get her ass in gear. While the beast was delighted with all the play time, it was out of shape and nearing its physical limit.

She used the last bit of energy she possessed and leapt forward, which drew a groan of frustration from Kade. She laughed inside, not only at how much fun the night had been, but also at her idiocy. How could she have ever doubted Kade was her mate? It was so obvious now. He was her one and only, her destiny. Just one more thing Brian had lied about. At least her heart *and* head finally knew the truth.

Barking with joy—and maybe to taunt Kade a little—she dug her claws into the ground harder with every frenzied step. The trees grew closer and closer, but through the latticework of branches she could just make out the blazing porch light in the distance. They were nearly to the pack house. If she could make it there before him, she could hold it over his head for the rest of their lives. The perfect way to start their life together!

Kade was hot on her heels when she broke through the tree line and into the clearing. Then a familiar scent caused her to falter. Kade whizzed past, but Ally barely noticed. All of her attention was on the smell of rotting garbage and wet dog.

Brian.

Locking her legs, she skidded to a stop and sniffed the air. He'd definitely been there recently. Pressing her nose to the ground, she caught his trail, pausing just long enough to bark a warning at Kade. He slowed, joy emanating off him in waves, and cocked his head. She barked again, this time more urgently, and returned her attention to following Brian's trail.

She was halfway past the pack house when Kade caught up with her, snuffling the ground in her wake. He knew Brian's scent and immediately sent up a shrill howl. A chill set the fur along her spine on end. It was a warning cry, a cry for help. She'd never heard it before, but she knew it immediately.

The world around them went silent—no yips of joy, no barks of pleasure, even the crickets quieted—then exploded. His cry was answered by dozens more and the forest erupted with the sounds of wolves crashing toward them.

Ally barely spared them any attention. She no longer needed to urge her wolf to move faster. Her wolf moved with a lithe agility she'd never known she possessed. Over stumps, beneath branches, through underbrush, nothing slowed her down. She couldn't allow anything to delay her. Whatever Brian was up to, it wasn't bound to be a sweet mating gift for her and Kade.

She soon sensed others join the search. Everyone had been warned about an intruder so they'd all responded to protect the pack. She would have fought Brian on her own, if necessary, but she'd been on the receiving end of his insanity in the past and she wouldn't survive it again.

The longer they ran, the more concentrated the scent became. Bile rose in the back of her throat as the rotten fruit scent of him clung to the fine hairs inside her nose. Just as she was about to retch, she caught a new scent on the air and her blood went cold.

Sweet like chocolate, with a hint of cayenne. Little Charlie Tipton, bundle of energy, owner of Ghost Kitty, and her second favorite Blackwood wolf. His scent was strong, panic mixed in with his natural aroma.

Brian had Charlie.

Ally growled with a new wave of rage. She continued to

follow Brian's path. Pushing, pushing, pushing, she paid no attention to branches cutting through her fur and drawing blood. She had to find Charlie, *had* to!

The scents faded, so Ally veered to the right and caught them once more, stronger and fresher than ever. They remained mixed as the pack hunted the pair, dread weighing her down with every step. Crashing into a clearing, Ally skidded to a stop, followed by the rest of the Blackwood pack.

Brian had left her a gift after all—one so horrible he was the only person disgusting enough to dream it into reality.

Charlie, in human form, sat chained by the neck to a massive tree, frothing at the mouth and snarling like a rabid dog. As more and more wolves entered the small area, Charlie went into an absolute frenzy, shifting from human to wolf and back again. The young boy gnashed his teeth and snarled at them. Blood trickled down his little chest from the cruel iron collar clamped around his neck. His brown eyes rolled into the back of his head, leaving only the whites.

Ally froze, recalling a similar scene years earlier. Only she'd been the one shackled to a tree.

Overcome by the power of the memory she'd suppressed for eight long years, Ally shifted to her human form as she crumpled to the ground, a quivering mess. She couldn't tear her gaze away, knowing exactly how the boy was feeling as he clawed at his own neck to free himself—or to escape the agony of his own skin. The sting of the metal was nothing compared to the confusion, desperation and all-consuming rage that flooded him. She'd tried to forget about that night but seeing Charlie's suffering brought it all back on a tsunami of emotion.

Through a veil of tears, Ally crawled toward the boy, heedless of Kade's human presence by her side. She needed to reach Charlie, help him. But her path was blocked by the largest wolf she'd ever seen. The smell of his fury filled the clearing. He bounded into the clearing and headed straight for Charlie, shifting mid-stride. Before Ally could crawl more than a couple of feet, Mason had reached the boy and was reaching for the collar.

"No!" she choked out, but it was too late.

The moment Charlie, now in a rabid wolf form, was set free from his bonds, he lunged for Mason's throat. The man's lightning-fast reflexes saved his life as he brought up his arm just in time for Charlie's fangs to bury deep in his flesh. The pup shook his head, as any canine did when trying to kill its prey, tearing chunks of Mason's arm free.

Mason remained silent, but Ally knew that wouldn't last. Bracing herself for the inevitable retribution, Ally clamped her eyes shut. If she knew anything about wolf packs, it was that no Alpha would tolerate being attacked by one of his subordinates, even a pup. Punishment would be swift and merciless. She couldn't bear to watch poor

Charlie be beaten—or worse—when none of this was his own doing. She'd learned that reasoning with Alphas rarely worked. The best she could do was help pick up the pieces later.

She waited for Charlie's yelp of pain, but it never came. She dared to open one eye and found that instead of beating the pup into submission, Mason and other pack members worked together to gently subdue the boy.

Lucy called out for Drew, the pack healer, as well a woman named Mathilda, the pack's Omega, if Ally remembered right. The clearing became a bustle of activity, with several people holding Charlie as he frothed and fumed. Kade's brother Gavin organized search teams to track down the intruder and set up a perimeter to keep the women and children safe in the pack house.

A whirl of movement. A rapid response for the benefit of all.

Ally watched in wonder as the Blackwood pack not only worked hard to save the smallest among them, even after he viciously attacked the Alpha, but also worked as a team to protect the entire pack and its land. Kade hadn't been lying to her. This really was what a healthy pack looked like.

Once Drew arrived to examine Charlie, Mason leveled a murderous glare at Kade. "Find the motherfucker who did this," he growled.

All the fine hairs on Ally's body stood on end, and she knew the time for remaining silent about her past was over. She was part of this pack now—or would be as soon as she and Kade finally mated—and she couldn't allow anyone to suffer the way she had, no matter how painful or difficult the telling might be.

"Mason," she barely whispered, but she had the alpha's attention in an instant. "I know who did this. And I know what kind of poison he used."

CHAPTER EIGHTEEN

ALLY STARED INTO HER CUP OF CHAMOMILE TEA UNTIL HER
head swam. She wasn't thirsty, and the hot mug burned
her palms, but it gave her something to do. Something to
focus on while they waited for word on Charlie. Plus,
staring into the pale yellow liquid gave her a reason to not
meet anyone's gaze.

"I feel just terrible," Tessa moaned and buried her face in
her hands.

"Grandma, stop beating yourself up." Lucy continued to
gently rub the old woman's back. "You were asleep when
Charlie left the pack house."

"That's my point!" Tessa cried, and her voice trembled
with emotion. "He was in my care. I should have watched
him more closely."

Gavin sat on the coffee table in front of Tessa and patted

her knee. "No one expected you to keep an eye on the pups every minute. Pups play outside at night all the time, Tessa, and you needed your sleep. You couldn't have known about the intruder. Hell, *we* didn't know, and we're werewolves."

Lucy wrapped a comforting arm around Tessa's shoulders. "He's right, Grandma."

"I just hope he'll be okay," Tessa said, her voice sounding frailer than Ally had ever heard.

"He should be," said a deep, booming voice from behind them.

Mason strode into the great room, his expression tense and grim, but not grieving. Ally's heart fluttered with hope that poor, little Charlie might have been spared the worst of the poison.

"Drew and Mathilda are with him now. Drew is our healer, Grandmother Tessa, and Mathilda is our Omega. She's something of an empath, and she'll help control his heart rate and mood, while Drew tends to his wounds. They're both optimistic Charlie will make a full recovery, thanks to Ally telling us what kind of poison he'd been dosed with."

Ally felt five pairs of eyes bore into her, but she kept her attention fixed on the swirling remnants of chamomile at the bottom of her cup. She knew it wasn't her fault Brian had kidnapped Charlie—it was Brian's—but that didn't stop her conscience from telling her otherwise.

"What was it?" Gavin asked.

"It was formulated in the '60s and was meant to break down prisoners—make them docile. The National Ruling Circle banned it, but apparently some vials weren't destroyed. I spoke with Roman—he's the Alpha of the NRC, Grandmother Tessa—and it appears the same stuff was used on the Alpha of another pack here in Georgia. He also gave us the recipe for the antidote."

"Oh, thank God!" Tessa flopped back in her chair and smiled up at Lucy.

Ally felt Mason's gaze settle on her as he sat directly across from her. She couldn't resist looking up at him. He was her Alpha now, after all.

"Speak."

She'd promised them the truth and it was time to deliver, no matter how difficult it would be. Her heart rate ratcheted up higher and higher with every second she delayed. Best to simply begin. Before she could, Kade's fingers laced with hers, giving her the strength she desperately needed.

"I'm—" her voice shook, and she cleared her throat before starting again. "I'm from a small town just outside

Brookfield, Alabama. I have two parents who, as far as I know, are still madly in love, and a twin sister."

Lucy's eyes widened, but she remained silent, allowing Ally to continue her story.

"I left home at eighteen and came to Georgia to go to college. My sister had a high school sweetheart who'd gone to trade school, so she stayed home to be with him." Ally swallowed, remembering the pain of being separated from her twin for the first time. It seemed like a lifetime ago now. "It was a hard time, being separated from my best friend like that. Amy and I were inseparable our entire lives, and then she was just gone. Or rather, *I* was gone. Without her, I had no idea what to do with myself. Not only was I alone, I was lonely."

"You had me," Lucy said, sitting on Ally's other side and clasping her free hand. "You always will."

She smiled at her friend, although it probably looked more like a grimace. "I know. But you had your own life and friends. At best, we were acquaintances back then. It wasn't until we bumped into each other in Pepper that we finally grew close."

With the foundation laid, now came the hard part. Building the story, one brick at a time. "One day, I was in the library cramming for a test. I needed a caffeine boost, so I popped over to the campus coffee shop. The place was crowded, and there were often local kids who'd come and visit their friends. I'd never met the guy in line behind me, but he bought my coffee and asked me out on a date. He was handsome, a little older than me, and the first guy at school who'd shown any interest in me. I agreed before I'd even realized what I'd done."

Even now, after all that had happened, the memory gave her warm fuzzies. She'd never actually been hit on before, and it had made her feel... pretty. "We dated for a few months and grew more and more serious. One night he took me out to a fancy dinner, gave me roses, the whole shebang. For a minute I thought he might propose, which I can't deny excited me a little. It also freaked me out a little because we'd only been dating a short time."

"Did he?" Lucy's voice was soft.

"No, but he did tell me he was in love with me. I was so relieved he wasn't proposing that I told him I loved him too. Looking back, I was so young I don't think I really knew what love was at the time."

She turned to Kade, who gathered her in his arms and held on tight for the rest of the story. "To celebrate, he invited me to go on a romantic weekend camping trip on his family's land. Just the two of us hiking under the full moon across the Riverson's beautiful property."

The sharp scent of tension filled the room. Everyone's eyes, except Tessa's, grew wide, but Ally had no idea what she'd said to trigger the mood change.

"What?"

Mason leaned forward, his eyes blazing. "Did you say Riverson? Your boyfriend was…"

"Brian Riverson. Do you know him?" Ally tilted her head to the side with the question. The werewolf community was small enough that it shouldn't have come as a surprise, yet it still did.

"He used to be my best friend," Gavin spoke just as softly, his face pale with obvious shock. He rose from the coffee table and moved to a seat on the couch. "Haven't seen him since…"

No one spoke. Ally looked between them, but each looked as dumbfounded as the last. "Since when? Someone please tell me what's going on."

"Brian's father, Frank, was the Alpha of the Riverson pack," Mason explained quietly. "Frank's mate went feral. As the Alpha, it was his duty to… for lack of a better term, put her down before innocents were hurt. He didn't."

A flicker of a memory tried to push forward into Ally's brain, but she wanted to give every ounce of her attention to what they were saying about Brian. Mason glanced at Tessa, then at Lucy, as if asking her a silent question. Lucy's pretty face pinched up, then she gave a curt nod and took over.

"It seems that a number of Riverson pack mates knew

what was happening to Kathy, but no one stopped her. They let her roam around until she stumbled across some campers."

Tessa gasped and clamped her hands over her mouth, and Ally's skin pebbled as understanding dawned. Lucy lunged across the space to hold her trembling grandmother in her arms as Mason finished the grim tale.

"Frank watched from the shadows as his mate murdered Lucy's parents and mauled her."

"Oh, Lucy, Tessa, I'm so sorry," Ally whispered, and reached out a hand to her friend.

They clasped hands for a moment, then Lucy went back to comforting her grandmother. Ally couldn't imagine Tessa's shock at discovering exactly how her son and daughter-in-law had died.

"Frank was imprisoned by the NRC for a decade and his pack was forced to disband. Most of the pack chose to integrate into others, including ours. Those who did have thrived."

Ally's voice shook when she spoke. "Wait, he only went away for ten years?"

Mason heaved a frustrated sigh. "Psychopaths are pretty good at fooling even the most astute Omegas. He was released from prison shortly before Lucy and I found each other. When he came back seeking vengeance for his mate, Lucy…"

He glanced over at Lucy again. She gave him a soft look filled with love, then turned to Ally.

"I killed him. With a hoe. To protect Mason."

"Good!" Tessa spit, tears tracing the tracks of her wrinkled cheeks. "I hope he rots in hell with his bitch wife!"

Lucy hugged Tessa tighter, and a fresh wave of anger hit Ally. Brian's family had been responsible for shattering Lucy and Tessa's hearts, forever changing their lives for the worse. And now he wanted to do the same to Ally.

"I guess insanity runs in the family," she snapped, then gasped as the memory that had been floating around came into full view. "Oh my God!"

"What?" Mason demanded.

"I think I know why Brian's mother went feral. Let me finish my story and maybe it will all make sense."

Kade squeezed her hand, a silent reminder that he was still by her side and always would be. It gave her the strength to carry on.

"The moonlight hike was romantic, and we had a nice evening before setting up our tents. I'd brought my own because Brian and I hadn't… Anyway, I woke up in the middle of the night and Brian was lying on his side next to me, unzipping my sleeping bag. In my sleepy daze, I thought he just wanted to make out a little, so I didn't put up much of a fuss, but then…"

She blindly reached for Kade's hand as she remembered Brian's groping hands on her body and the sudden jolt of fear when he ignored her protests.

"The bottom line is he tried to rape me. He kept calling me his mate and that it was destiny we should be together and a bunch of other bullshit."

"Oh fuck," Kade breathed just loud enough for her to hear, and she knew he finally understood her original suspicions of him. Kade had said the same things Brian had claimed as he was trying to rape her.

"I managed to stick my thumbs in his eyes hard enough that he screamed and rolled off. I scrambled out of the tent and ran for my life, but not fast enough. The last thing I really remember is being tackled by a huge wolf and the pain when his fangs sank into my neck."

"Jesus," Gavin breathed.

"I don't remember much about the next few days—at least I think that's how long it took me to recover—except excruciating pain. I do recall flashes of someone, a female, who remained by my side through all of it, soothing me. Not that she helped much. I was so certain I was dying, I thought I heard death calling me. And I can't deny that I wanted to go."

"You must be exceptionally strong not to have died," Gavin said.

"She is," Lucy said, tears streaming down her face now, a younger version of Tessa. "I nearly died from a pup bite, which *must* be less potent than a full-grown male's bite."

She shot a glance at Mason, who nodded. Not that Ally cared, not anymore. All the mattered now was finding Brian and stopping him from hurting anyone else.

"When I finally became lucid, Brian paid me a visit. I'll never forget the look of revulsion on his face when he stepped in the room and smelled the truth. 'You're not my mate!' he shouted. Then he dragged me from my deathbed and beat me until I passed out."

Ally's chest constricted. She'd never told another living soul about Brian, and though she felt disconnected from that long ago trauma, the simple act of speaking about it brought a fresh wave of pain. She would push through, but not without stirring up shit she'd spent eight years trying to forget.

"He spent the next few months punishing me for not being his mate. It didn't matter to him in the slightest that he'd changed me for no reason. In fact, he said another female could always be useful to the pack."

The scent of Kade's outrage drifted over her. She almost pitied Brian, because her mate wouldn't stop hunting until he tracked down her attacker and justice had been served.

"What pack?" Mason asked.

Ally snorted. "That's what Brian called it, but it was really just a motley crew of scumbags who'd been banished from their own packs. From what you said, a large chunk were probably Riverson wolves. I hated every last one of them, but we had one thing in common. We were all terrified of Brian."

"Regardless, I can't believe no one helped you," Lucy said, reaching a hand over to clasp Ally's. "I always wondered why you'd dropped out of school."

Ally smiled at her friend. "I didn't so much 'drop out' as 'disappear'. And I didn't expect any of them to help me. Brian hated me for not being his fated mate, and we all knew what would happen if anyone was caught being kind to me. Except Rachel. She was the one who helped me through my change, and if my guess is right, she was an Omega. She tried to stand up for me a few times, only to suffer dearly as a result. I eventually insisted she stop. I couldn't take the guilt."

Ally had often thought about Rachel over the years and wondered if she'd ever made it out of Brian's pack alive.

"Of course, none of that stopped me from trying to escape. I probably broke free at least a dozen times, and almost made it to safety on three different occasions before some slavering asshole hunted me down. After the last time, Brian said he knew what would tame me. I

CELIA KYLE & MARINA MADDIX

remember him saying it hadn't worked on his rebellious mother, but his father had left a supply hidden on their lands, just in case."

As her words sank in, the others exchanged shocked glances. Lucy gasped and started shaking. This time it was Tessa's turn to comfort her granddaughter.

"So that's why Kathy went feral," Mason mused. "That's always bothered me. It's very rare for mated wolves to lose their minds like that."

Lucy turned a furious gaze on Ally. "Are you telling me Frank Riverson didn't just stand by while his mate attacked us, but he was directly responsible for making her crazy in the first place?"

"I think so," Ally said.

"Hmph." Lucy glared out the window at nothing in particular. "Now I don't feel so bad about bashing his skull in with the business end of a hoe."

"What did he do, Ally?" Kade asked, his voice carefully controlled, but she could hear the quaver of rage behind it.

"He chained me to a tree, just like he did to Charlie. Then he forced a vial of nasty liquid down my throat. I can almost taste its bitterness now."

"It acted on you the same as it did on Charlie?" Mason asked.

Ally nodded. "The mania almost took me. I remember him saying he was going to give me half a dose because he didn't want to repeat his father's mistake. I guess it wasn't enough."

"Maybe your uncommon strength is what helped you survive," Gavin said with a hint of admiration in his voice.

"Whatever the reason, my mind cleared enough to understand what happened. They'd left me out there all alone, waiting for me to either become docile or die. Once I was able to use reason *and* my new strength, I broke free and never looked back."

She laughed bitterly, lips curled in a sneer while she shook her head. "That's not true. Since that night eight years ago, I've constantly looked over my shoulder, waiting for him to find me. I knew I could never see my family again. Rachel had told me my 'death' had been widely reported in the news. A search party had discovered my shredded clothes and my blood, and that was enough for the authorities to declare I'd been the victim of an animal attack. If I returned from the dead, it would definitely make the news and he'd find me. I had to stay away from my parents and sister, for their own safety."

"So where did you go?" Lucy asked.

"Underground. I moved around a lot, took commitment-free jobs, kept my wolf in submission, and kept a go bag in my trunk at all times. I didn't understand the wolf inside me or how to handle it, so I rarely released it."

"That might have helped save your sanity," Gavin said. "Any other wolf in that situation would have gone feral. No pack? No Alpha? No mate?" He let out a low whistle.

A whiff of Kade's jealousy caught her attention. He didn't like her getting attention from another male, so she squeezed his hand to calm him again before continuing.

"Every time I even *thought* Brian might be closing in, I ran. Then I landed in Pepper and found Tessa and Lucy…" She sniffled. "I'm not sure I can express in words the pain I suffered in leaving my family behind, especially my sister. I would have gone through the change and the poison a thousand times just to see them once more. So, when I bumped into Lucy and she remembered me… I knew I'd found my new sister. You two were my foster family. After so long on my own, I couldn't leave you."

Lucy and Tessa were full-on sobbing, right along with Ally.

"I'm so sorry for bringing Brian into your lives, for putting you both in jeopardy. Putting you *all* in jeopardy. When I realized he'd found me in Pepper, I went with Kade in the hopes that I'd finally be safe—at least long enough to make another escape. I never expected him to find me again so soon. He must have kidnapped Charlie to prove his point. To show me I'll never be safe."

She brushed away her tears, then turned to Kade. "Deep down, my wolf knew the truth of our bond, but it took my brain longer to accept it. I would never have knowingly put you in danger and I'm so sorry." With one final shaky breath, she turned to Mason. Bracing herself, she said, "This is all my fault, and I'm going to fix it."

CHAPTER NINETEEN

KADE HAD SAT NEXT TO ALLY, SILENTLY SUPPORTING HER through her story, but now that she was done, he couldn't sit still for one more second. Jumping to his feet, he balled up his fists and stalked into the kitchen. He needed to think, away from the intoxicating scent of his mate and the rage he'd been suppressing.

She'd dropped enough clues over the previous few days for him to catch on that she'd been hurt, maybe abused, but suspecting was one thing. Knowing every evil detail of what that bastard had done…

His wolf snarled, and white-hot anger flashed before his eyes. He wanted to punch a wall—or better yet, find that sonofabitch and rip out his motherfucking throat. No, that was too quick, too easy.

When he found Brian Riverson, Kade would cut him into

tiny pieces. Slowly. Carefully. Inflicting as much pain as possible, which would still be less than the coward deserved. He would start with Brian's toes, so his captive had a ringside view of the action. By the time Kade was done with him, the asshole would understand pain like no one else in the history of the universe.

"What are you doing in here?"

Kade jumped and spun around to find Mason standing in the doorway. He'd been so engrossed in his thoughts of revenge, his senses had failed him. Some protector he'd turned out to be.

"I just needed a minute," he said through gritted teeth.

"I get it bro." Mason moved forward and threw an arm over Kade's tense shoulders.

"I'm going to kill him, Mason. I'm going to do worse than kill him."

"He needs to be put down," Mason agreed, "but not right now."

Kade balked and opened his mouth to object, but Mason cut him off.

"Brian's time will come, trust me. Right now, you have a mate to soothe and protect. Why don't you take her up to one of the guest rooms and get some sleep? She's going to be wrecked after all of this."

Kade's cock thought being alone with Ally was an excellent idea, while his brain thought his cock was a total asshole. His mate had just revealed a dark and violent past and his first thought was getting inside of her.

Pathetic.

With a deep breath, Kade finally nodded. "Thanks, Mason."

"Hey, what are brothers for if not to tell you when you're being an idiot?"

Kade cracked a smile. "I may never know."

Back in the great room, Tessa and Lucy flanked Ally on the couch, holding each other for comfort. One look told him Mason had been right. She looked drained. Even so, when she met his gaze and gave him a weary smile, his heart beat double-time.

Striding to her, he held out a hand. "Come on, let's go get some rest."

"Okay," she sighed, as if the mere *thought* of moving exhausted her. "Although I'm warning you right now that you'll have to carry me at least half the way back to your place."

Helping her up, he led her to the main staircase. "Let's just grab a guest room upstairs."

"That sounds perfect."

Kade led her to the guest room at the end of the hall. This one featured an attached bathroom where they could wash off the sweat and dirt of the night before. Kade bustled around the room, preparing the bathroom with a fluffy robe, towel and washcloth while he turned on the shower.

Ally flopped back on the bed with a soft sigh. "God, this bed feels like heaven."

Kade chuckled. "You rest while I grab a shower."

"God, a shower sounds like heaven!"

This time he laughed outright. "Ladies first. I'll go back downstairs "

"No." Her voice was soft, but firm. "Stay."

Kade refused to let his mind wander into dangerous territory again. Ally was exhausted and needed rest, not recreation.

"Whatever you want." He slumped into a comfy chair in the corner.

Sitting up, she reached for the buttons of her shirt, fingers shaking as she unfastened each one slowly. Kade averted his gaze to give her some privacy, but even the sound of her clothes falling away set his pulse racing.

"You can watch, if you want," she almost whispered.

Kade met her gaze just as her shorts slipped to the floor,

leaving her in nothing but her white lace panties and matching bra. She stood boldly, but her hands twitched, and he knew she wanted to cover her tummy.

"Kade?"

"Hmm?" He could barely focus on her words with her standing in front of him almost naked.

"Now that you know the truth about me, about my past," she started, a tremor in her voice that brought his gaze back to hers. "Now that you know how weak I am, do you still want me as your mate?"

She'd barely spoken the words and Kade was out of his seat, standing in front of her. "Of course, I do. Gavin's right. It takes a strong person—hell, a strong wolf—to survive all you've been through. You're not weak, Ally. You're supremely powerful and I'm so amazed and proud of you. Proud to call you my mate."

Kade sniffed away the tingles that pricked the backs of his eyes. It wouldn't do for his mate to see him crying like a baby.

A delicate smile lit her face. "Do you really mean that?"

"Every word."

In response, she looped her hand behind her back and twisted the clasp of her bra, letting it fall to the floor in front of her as she shimmied out of her panties — all the while keeping her eyes locked on his. Once again, she laid herself bare to him. He swallowed hard, his mind struggling to understand how so much strength and beauty could live inside one person.

"Come on," she said, stepping past him and heading for the bathroom.

Kade stayed put and closed his eyes, counting to ten. He wanted to be a good guy, let her do her thing without any pressure for physical intimacy, even though every nerve was ablaze. Then she poked her head around the corner and smiled.

"You coming?"

He shook his head, despite his cock and wolf both protesting the injustice of it all. "You've been through so much. Right now, you need—"

"I know what I need right now," she cut in, then walked toward him, her breasts bouncing as she moved. She gripped the hem of his shirt and slowly dragged it over his head.

"Ally," he whispered, but she silenced him with a soft kiss.

"After everything you've seen and heard, you still want me. Kade, I'm never letting you get away. If I'm yours, then you're mine."

Her mouth dropped to the base of his neck and he wondered if she could feel the hard thrum of his heart against her lips. His cock ached as it strained against his jeans, but he repressed his urge to growl.

"You should take it easy."

She growled against his skin in frustration, sending tremors of need through his body, then stepped back and cocked her head in a challenge.

"Get in the shower, Kade." She spun around, giving him a perfect view of her perfect ass. Pausing at the bathroom doorway, she flipped her long hair and glanced over her shoulder at him. She looked every bit a pinup girl. "I've got a mate to claim, but that can't happen if he doesn't do his part."

CHAPTER TWENTY

THE BATHROOM WAS ALMOST AS BIG AS THE BEDROOM, THE design a mixture of the rustic charm throughout the house but tempered with a softer edge. It beckoned her onward, encouraging her to rest, relax, and enjoy herself... Maybe it was the early morning sun casting the glass shower in an ethereal glow. Or the bronze chandelier that hung from the ceiling over the double-slipper clawfoot tub, its bulbs giving the nook a subtle radiance.

Perhaps it was sensual simply because she was in a safe place, moments from being claimed by her mate.

Kade's steps were silent as he crossed the bedroom and joined her, the bathroom door closing with a soft *snick*. Then his heat was there, body close enough to warm her back, yet he didn't touch her.

"Ally," he murmured, his breath fanning her shoulder.

He pressed a kiss to her skin, just a chaste brushing of his lips on her, but it felt so much more intimate. As if he explored the most sensual parts of her instead of merely her shoulder. She shuddered, a jolt of desire slithering through her veins, and her pussy clenched with need.

"You don't have to be nervous." Kade nuzzled her neck, a rough scrape of his shadowy beard over her sensitive skin. "I'd never do anything to hurt you and the water won't allow anyone to hear us."

Ally shook her head. "I'm not nervous and I don't care if anyone hears us."

Steam drifted over the glass-enclosed shower and she breathed deep, loving the mix of soothing warm mist and the scents of their combined desire. Her nipples strained, hardening to firm points despite the heat. Ally turned, her breasts nearly brushing Kade's bare chest, and she couldn't keep her hands to herself. She reached for him, pulling him closer until there was no space between their bodies.

"I want this to be exactly how you want it to be—everything you've ever dreamed." Kade's gaze met hers, his stare intent and searching.

"I never dreamed of something like this. I never dreamed..." She swallowed hard, the pain of the past fighting to ruin this moment. "If I'm with you, then this is how it's meant to be."

Ally pressed to her tiptoes and gave Kade a teasing, chaste kiss, but pulled back before he could take over and deepen the connection. She eased away and slowly, ever so slowly, she lowered to her knees. Her wolf rumbled, happy with the series of events. Even happier when she flicked the snap of his jeans and lowered the fly. The zipper parted to reveal the dark blue boxer briefs he wore beneath the rough fabric.

Her hands shook with anticipation... need... lust. She grasped the waist of his pants and tugged, pulling until they slumped to the floor. Kade's thick fingers slipped into her hair, large palm cupping her skull. His boxers remained in place, the only thing keeping him hidden from view.

"Ally," he murmured, and she absorbed the way he said her name—wanted to remember it and cherish it for all time.

Gripping the waist of his boxers, she tugged on the elastic and carefully slid them down, allowing his hard length to spring forward. Once again, her breath caught at the sight of his cock—further proof of his need.

"Mmmm..." She licked her lips, mouth watering. She traced the line of dark hair that led from his belly button and right to his rigid need.

"Like what you see?"

She nodded, lips quirked. "Why don't I show you how much?"

Ally wrapped her hand around his shaft, silken heat beneath her palm—so soft yet so very hard. She stroked his length, gliding along that sensitive, private part of him. Up and down, base to tip and back again, she took her time while pleasuring her mate. He released a low groan, free hand reaching out to brace himself on the counter while the other remained knotted in her hair. He panted, chest heaving, as she explored his cock. Thick and hard, the plum-shaped tip flushed with his arousal.

"You like that?" she whispered, lips just brushing the head of his dick.

"You have no idea." The words held a hint of his wolf, a rumbling growl in each syllable. "Just to feel your skin—"

Ally silenced by him flicking out her tongue and lapping up the droplet of pre-cum that leaked from his length. She savored the salty essence of her mate and went back for more. She rolled the tip of her tongue over him, tapping the slit at the tip and capturing each new morsel as it left him. He jerked and quaked at her touches, hips twitching when she laved the underside of his dick, teasing that sensitive spot before moving on once more.

She cupped his balls, massaging him as she took him into her mouth. She slid her lips along his hardness, tracing the veins with her tongue as she took in more of him. She bobbed once, twice, slow and easy—sensual. She ached for him to spill in her mouth but this was only the start of everything she wanted to give him.

"Ally," he groaned. "I need you."

God, she needed him too, and it took every ounce of control she had to remain on her knees. In answer to his plea, she gripped the base of his shaft and took as much of him in her mouth as she could—until the hard head of his cock bumped the back of her throat.

"Fuck," he ground out, and she hummed in approval before she retreated until she reached the head once more. Then she began the torturous game of sliding her tongue around his tip, teasing the flared edge, tapping the underside, and lapping up every drop of pre-cum.

"You're going to kill me, woman," Kade snarled, but there was no heat in the sound. Simply sexual need and frustration.

She eased back enough to speak, but refused to relinquish her treat entirely. Her lips brushed the sensitive tip as she spoke. "And you'll love every moment."

Kade's grip in her hair tightened as she took him deep once more, humming as she slid up, then down and up again. She breathed deep through her nose, relishing the musky scent of wolf and male. She reveled in the way she sensed the unrelenting need pouring off him in drowning waves. She would never doubt the way he felt about her. It oozed from every pore, and the depth increased her own. The pressure and aching desperation between her thighs rose higher and higher until she felt as if she'd burst into flame.

Ally swallowed him down once again, not stopping until he nudged the back of her throat, and she paused for a moment—simply holding him in her mouth. His taste... His closeness... She gradually retreated, withdrawing in slow increments until she reached the head. She was prepared for more teasing—more delicate licking and exploring with her tongue—but Kade refused to allow her torment to continue.

Kade jerked his cock away and bent, grasping her biceps before hauling her to her feet. His hold was firm as he moved her, encouraging her to move backward until she was pressed against the damp tiled wall. The bathroom had become more sauna than anything, the steaming shower continuing to toss moisture into the air. The cool tile was a stark contrast to the warmth enveloping.

With the wall at her back, she had nowhere to go as Kade continued to come forward, not stopping until his chest was flush with hers—his cock nudging her hip.

"What's wrong?" Her heart thrummed a rapid beat, though they were so close she wondered if it was his heart.

"Not a damned thing." Kade crushed his mouth over hers,

sucking on her bottom lip for a moment before delving into her mouth. He cupped her cheek, other hand still in her hair and holding her just as he desired. She squirmed against the wall, fighting to push closer, to press up into his mouth and lose herself in him. She drank him in with every breath, savoring every hint of his scent.

Even when she'd lost her composure the first night, she'd never imagined a kiss could be this *good*. No, Good wasn't enough. It was simply perfect. So full of craving and want and understanding. His mouth crashed against hers, moving in undulating waves of push and pull, need and fleeting satisfaction warring inside her. At that moment, she felt as though she was more than herself. Or more than *just* her.

She was Kade, too. His all-consuming desperation to take her nearly making her lose control. A yearning she experienced as well. Somehow, they knew each other better than they knew themselves, bodies and minds exchanging information on a level she couldn't comprehend. He sensed what she craved even before the thought fully formed, just as she knew what he desired without him saying a word.

The hand at her cheek abandoned her, traveling down her body and settling at the juncture of her thighs. He found her slick folds, fingers not hesitating to explore that sensitized part of her. He rolled his thumb over her clit, mimicking the pattern he used with his tongue in her mouth. He fucked her with his hand, fingers not missing an inch of her pussy as he discovered her secrets.

She rolled her hips, rocking against him in her quest for that ultimate pleasure. She rode his fingers as if it were his cock filling her, gasping with bone-deep relief with his sensual touch.

"Kade," she whimpered, voice tight with need, "My Kade."

It had all happened in a space of minutes but the anticipation had built over days. Days of looks and touches and secret smiles. Of heated stares that held so much promise.

Ally found herself soaring higher, body taken away by Kade's delicious ministrations. He fucked her hard and slow, plunging deep into her pussy as his thumb traced tormenting circles around her clit. She gasped and whined, working with him, taking everything she could. Their mouths remained connected, the kiss continuing as his taunting seemed never ending.

The pleasure spiraled higher, flying upward and climbing toward the precipice. Kade delved deep, taking cues from her until he repeated everything that made her moan and doubled whatever movements made her scream his name against his lips.

And still the bliss gathered and grew, the bubble of restrained passion swelling around her. Her nipples pebbled against his chest and her pussy clenched around his invasion, milking his fingers just as she'd like to milk the hard length of his cock.

Soon...

"Kade," she panted. "Oh, god, Kade…." Ally pulled out of the kiss and slumped against the wall, mewling and whining for more.

"Tell me. Say it. What do you want?"

Ally's fingers twitched and hands raised to her breasts, pinching the tight nubs of her nipples without thought. All the while, his ministrations remained, the delirious rhythm not stuttering in any way. A full-body tremor overtook her, that growing ecstasy expanding to creep into every inch of her.

"More. You. I want to come." Another shudder stole more of her control, sapping her of what little strength she had, and she found herself balancing on that edge. On that line between bone-searing pleasure and pain, and she held her breath, not wanting to interrupt that sensual dance. She wavered, body trembling, muscles no longer her own as Kade stole any hint of control she might have possessed.

He leaned forward, his cheek against hers, nuzzling her as his hot breath fanned her damp skin, his closeness adding to the intense joy coursing through her veins.

"Ally." Kade's dark rasp was all she needed.

Her pussy clenched around his thick fingers,

convulsions snatching any hint of control that remained. Utter bliss consumed her, the pleasure so intense she couldn't breathe. She shuddered and moaned, Kade's name on her lips as she flew apart in his arms. She rolled her hips in time with the hot, hard waves of ecstasy, another throb pulsing through her veins with every beat of her heart.

Ally's fangs pushed through her gums, descending until the sharp tips pricked her lower lip. Her wolf knew what it wanted—what it craved—and the beast made sure she was aware. She didn't allow herself to think or second guess herself once again, she simply struck.

Overwhelming pleasure still consuming her blood, she lurched forward and sank her fangs into his flesh. Kade's warm, coppery yet sweet, blood filled her mouth and she swallowed the fluid, reveling in this new connection between them. He growled with her claiming, the sound so low and deep she felt his hum in her bones—in her very soul.

And nothing had ever felt so right.

ALLY RELEASED HIM SLOWLY, TEETH SLIDING FREE OF HIS flesh followed by her delicate tongue lapping at his new mating mark. With each flick of her tongue, his cock throbbed, body anxious to sink into her. To feel her silken pussy wrap around him like a glove. One made just for him.

She gave him one more, long, slow lick and he forced himself to step back—to put distance between them. If he didn't, he'd come right then and there.

He reached for his shoulder, fingers ghosting over the new wound, and he couldn't suppress the smile that overtook his lips. The wound still wept, but already it'd begun to heal, sure to leave a scar in its wake.

Ally remained leaning against the damp tile wall, her passion-filled gaze meeting his, her eyes now amber with the presence of her wolf.

"Aren't you going to claim me?" Her beast—not Ally's human half—asked the question.

"I will, little wolf, when I'm done with the rest of you." Kade sensed his own animal flare inside him, changing his vision for a split-second, which seemed to be enough for Ally's inner animal.

Entwining their fingers, he slid the shower door open with his free hand and then guided her inside the glass enclosure. He stepped aside to allow the warm water to sluice over her perfect, pert breasts, droplets clinging to her hardened nipples before falling to the tile below. He followed the trails of water down her body—eyes tracing every inch of her pale skin. Moving from her breasts to her tucked in waist and then the flare of her hips.

Hips he wanted to hold tight as he pounded into her. Hard. Fast. Until she screamed his name… again.

Leaving her beneath the spray, Kade moved around the glass enclosure, grasping the shampoo bottle as soon as he was close. He let the fragrant fluid pool in his palm and then he slowly, carefully lathered his fingers.

He stepped close to her once more, mere inches between their wet bodies, and he lowered his eyes to hers. "First, I'm going to take care of you." He reached for her hair and sank his fingers into the damp strands. "I'm going to slide my hands over every inch of your body. I want you relaxed, pampered, all soft and sweet and sexy." He massaged her scalp, smiling when her eyes fell closed and she dropped her head back. "Then I'm going to fuck you until you come so hard you don't even remember your own name."

Her breath caught followed by a low moan and a full body shudder. It took everything in him not to rush, everything in him to stay on task and pamper his gorgeous mate. He eased her back, the spray soaking her hair and washing the suds away.

"How does that sound, gorgeous?"

"It sounds like a lot of waiting," she whined.

He leaned down and nipped her shoulder, his fangs scraping her flushed skin. "The more you complain, the longer you'll have to wait."

The longer they'd *both* have to wait.

She made the motion to zip her lips shut then focused on him as he lathered his hands once more, this time with body wash.

"What if I want to touch you?" She stole some of his suds and slid her slick palms down his body, nearing his aching cock. He jerked at her intoxicating touch, closing his eyes for a moment to enjoy the sensation before pulling away.

"All in good time, my mate."

Kade took his time exploring her, beginning at her back, nibbling her neck before following each kiss with his soapy hands. He caressed her shoulders, large hands spanning her back with ease as he traced her spine with his thumbs. Then he reached the perfection of her ass, the pale, rounded curves seeming to beg for his touch.

He smoothed his hand over the mounds, fingers ghosting along the crack of her ass and teasing her dark cleft. She gasped and surprised him, arching her back and pushing into his touch—inviting him to explore.

Fuck, he want to do just that, but he held himself back. He'd come all over the shower floor. Instead, he dropped to his knees and lathered her toned, shapely calves, thighs and back to the curve of her hips.

"I think you missed a spot," she teased and he heard rather than saw her smile.

"What did I tell you about being impatient?"

Ally fell silent once again, but he sensed her need, the desperate ache to talk, to beg. He wanted to hear those cries, but not until they were both nearly mad with wanting.

Kade moved to her front, beginning once more at the slim line of her neck. He moved to the hollow of her collarbones and then her biceps and forearms before finally reaching her hands. Grasping them in his own, he encouraged her to place her palms on her own chest, to touch herself for him as the water continued to spray over warm skin. Her nipples were hard and flushed pink, too much of a temptation for him to deny, and he bent low to nip one and then the other. But he couldn't let himself get distracted. He guided her hands still lower.

Anticipation bubbled inside him, growing with every breath.

"What do you want me to do?"

"I think you know the answer to that question," he murmured in response, and he didn't recognize his own voice. He released her, letting her make the choice for herself.

Ally's gaze never leaving his, she slipped her fingers between her thighs, not hesitating to delve within her silky folds. The move was soon followed by a deep moan, her eyes fluttering at her own touch. Kade's balls throbbed and dick pulsed, the need to come nearly driving him mad.

"Are you wet? Are you ready for me?" His voice was more growl than man.

"Kade," she whispered.

"Is your pussy ready to be claimed?" The scent of her arousal filled the air, captured in the steam, and it surrounded him. It sank into his pores and blinded him to all else.

Shakily, she nodded, and he moved her as he desired once more. He placed one hand over hers, encouraging her to pleasure herself—to make small circles over her aching bud while he turned her to face the shower wall.

Ally braced one hand on the tile, the other still between her legs, still rubbing that bundle of nerves. She arched against him, plump ass gliding along his throbbing cock. He gritted his teeth and fought his orgasm back, forced his body to obey him when all he wanted was to lose himself with Ally.

"Please..." Ally's breathless voice cut through the patter of water against glass. Or maybe it was his imagination. He wasn't sure. He simply knew that he couldn't take it anymore. Couldn't take her nearness and not have her —claim her.

Kade grasped his shaft with his free hand and positioned

the tip of his cock at her hot, wet opening. Her pussy kissed the head of his dick, clenching as if hungry for him —to be claimed and filled by him. He didn't hesitate to answer her silent plea. He shoved hard and deep inside her, cock filling her pussy with that single thrust. She took him to the hilt, his entire length deep within her body until her ass was cradled by his hips.

He groaned deep, a low contrast to her high scream, the sounds ringing around them as they finally experienced what it was to be complete in each other's arms. Ally leaned back, her head going to his shoulder and her hair splayed against his chest.

He lowered his lips to her ear. "Don't stop touching yourself." He pressed his fingers hard against hers, punctuating his order with that extra push of sensation.

She gave him a shaky nod and he withdrew his hand, adjusting his hold gripping her hips. He withdrew and pushed forward once more, setting a slow rhythm as he simply reveled in the feel of her wrapped around him. Her sheath squeezed his length, rippling around him with every thrust, clinging to him as he retreated.

Ally met him stroke for stroke, rocking and pushing into his thrusts, taking everything he gave.

And then he gave her more, instincts and need driving him to thrust into her hard, slam their hips together, and pulling a cry from her throat. He thrust into her over and over and over… The only sounds in the shower coming from the patter of water and their hoarse cries.

Kade's gums ached, his wolf howling and pushing against its mental leash. It wanted freedom. It wanted to bite and claim as they'd already been claimed.

"*Kade.*" His name came out of Ally as a cross between a moan and a cry, begging and demanding at the same time. Then her pussy squeezed his cock, massaging his length, and his balls pulled up tight and hard against his body.

It was enough to wrench his focus away from corralling his beast and the wolf slipped its leash, transforming his fangs in an instant. They burst into his mouth, tips pricking his lower lip.

Ally braced her hand on the wall, using it to push against, shoving her body along his cock—using him, fucking herself on his dick and *fuck…*

She ached for him so much she was driven to fight for control. The perfect, needy little she-wolf.

Kade slammed into her hard, pushing her release higher, needing her to come on his cock before he sank his fangs into her flesh. They both fought for the same thing— release, that ultimate pleasure—and he knew when she was truly close. Knew when she hovered right at the edge. She trembled in his arms, muscles twitching and breathing coming in uneven gasps.

"Come, Ally." He pounded her again and again and again, not stopping. "Come on my cock and I'll claim you." Harder and harder still, his muscles straining and teeth clenched as he fought his own pinnacle. "Come and I'll fill you with my. Fucking. Scent."

He punctuated the words with sharp thrusts and then he knew she was there—body frozen, heartbeat stuttering, lungs no longer drawing in breath for a split-second. That was when she broke around him, shattered and gave into the pleasure. Which was his permission, all Kade needed to let himself go and let his inner beast snatch control.

Kade grunted as his balls went tight and cum snaked up his aching length, pouring unadulterated ecstasy through his veins. At the same moment he struck, mouth open and fangs bared. He bit into his mate's flesh, sinking his teeth deep and binding them as mates for the rest of their lives. He swallowed the sweet coppery blood that bubbled to the surface and filled his mouth, savoring the taste as it slid over his tongue.

All the while he fucked her. Fucked her through his orgasm and hers. Fucked her until the bleeding from her claiming mark slowed to no more than a trickle. Fucked her until not a drop of cum remained inside his body, his scent now coating his mate.

Bodies melded until he wasn't sure where he ended and she began and for the first time in his life, Kade felt... at peace.

CHAPTER TWENTY-ONE

ALLY WASN'T SURE IF SHE'D EVER FELT SO CONTENT. BEING near Kade, enjoying the outdoors, while he stood nearby and spoke with his brothers and a few other wolves… She'd never felt this way in her adult life. She had her mate and a pack that truly cared about her health and happiness.

As for the cherry on top of the ice cream sundae her life had become… that would be catching Brian.

Which was what the men discussed. It was the only thing anyone talked about since they'd found Charlie the morning before. They'd lost his trail and several enforcers had spent all day trying to sniff it out again, to no avail. Mason had decided the pack's Ruling Circle—he, Kade and Gavin—would join the hunt.

"We'll start where we found Charlie," he instructed the

group. "Emotions were wound up pretty tight yesterday, so we might have missed something."

"We might even get lucky and find the criminal has returned to the scene of the crime," Gavin said.

No one agreed.

Ally could smell the tension and anger, all the way from where she stood. It overpowered the travel cup of steaming coffee in her hands. Yet she remained strangely calm. That familiar creeping sense of dread that usually followed the mention of his name never surfaced.

Now that she'd been mated to Kade, her soul felt free and light—as if her wolf was finally in balance with the rest of her psyche. She had a pack now, a family bigger than any she'd ever known before, and a chance at happiness she'd never let herself hope for in the past

And it was all because of Kade.

She smiled at him—at her mate—enjoying the way his jeans accentuated his firm backside as he moved, and her wolf purred again at the thought of him. They'd sealed the bond between them in every way. If not for Brian, she would have been delirious with joy.

Anger flamed in her heart at what he'd done to sweet, innocent Charlie, and they were fanned by the guilt over her role in the matter. As the group of men climbed into their SUVs, Ally's faith that her new pack would find the bastard gave her a modicum of comfort.

She returned Kade's wave as the trucks sped off, then went and knocked on the pack house's front door. Kade had explained that she didn't need to knock every time, but she wasn't quite there yet. Almost before the last knock split the air, Mathilda cracked open the door.

"Ally, you never have to knock. Come in, come in." Mathilda glanced around behind her before opening the door wide. A kitten tried to bolt past, but the older woman blocked his escape with her foot. "Not so fast, little one!"

Ally hurriedly closed the door behind her and scooped the troublemaker into her arms. He was a tiny gray and white tuxedo kitty with a little dark splotch under his nose that looked like a mustache. The moment she tucked him against her chest, he started purring. *Loudly.*

"I think you have a new friend," Mathilda chuckled and led Ally down a long hallway. "You just missed Drew."

"And? What did he say?"

"He says Charlie is coming along nicely, though slower than he'd hoped." Mathilda's voice, along with her words, soothed Ally's worry a bit. "Thanks to your knowledge of what Charlie was poisoned with, Drew believes he administered the antidote in plenty of time avoid any permanent side effects. Unfortunately, the maniac who did this terrible thing gave Charlie an adult-sized dose."

Despite Mathilda's calming ways, the guilt crept back into Ally's heart. "It was probably meant for me. When he couldn't find me, he grabbed the easiest prey he could find."

Mathilda placed a soothing hand on Ally's shoulder as she opened a bedroom door. "Don't worry. It may be taking longer than expected, but Charlie will be back to terrorizing the pack in no time. Isn't that right, Charlie?"

The boy lay snuggled deep under the covers, his eyes transfixed on a handheld electronic game. When he looked up, Ally was nearly blinded by his beaming grin, once again amazed by how quickly children bounced back from illness.

"I'll leave you two alone." Mathilda gave Ally a quick wink.

Ally perched on the edge of the bed, careful not to jostle the young boy. "Hey champ, how are you feeling today?"

"Terrible! Mama won't let me have my comic books until after I finish my stupid homework. Doesn't she know I'm *sick?*"

"Yes, I can see your life is truly terrible," Ally drawled and raised a questioning eyebrow as she looked pointedly at the game in his hand. He gave her a sheepish smile and tucked it under his pillow. "You know, Charlie," Ally started cautiously, "I actually came by because I owe you an apology for putting you in danger. I'm so sorry for what happened."

The little boy's brows pulled low over his eyes. "You can't help what other people do. You can only help what you do, and you've always been nice to me."

Ally blinked at the wisdom in his words. "Did someone teach you that?"

"My mama."

"You've got a good mama—even though she makes you suffer without your comic books."

Charlie looked ready to agree, especially with the last part, when Mathilda popped her head back into the room.

"Will you be here for a few minutes, Ally?"

"I can be. What's up?"

Mathilda sighed. "One of our younger pups is having a little trouble controlling her shift this morning, which upsets her, which leads to even less control. I'd like to go calm her down. She can't very well go to school with a tail and wolf ears."

Charlie snickered, drawing a smile from Ally.

"Sure, Charlie and I have some catching up to do anyway. Isn't that right, champ?"

"I can show you my new game!"

"Great," Mathilda waved, chuckling as she disappeared from view.

As the woman's footsteps receded, Ally realized that *this* was what a healthy pack was supposed to be. Wolves caring and supporting one and other. Coming together in crisis. Protecting the pack.

Ally was one of them now, and none of them blamed her for what Brian did to Charlie. Not even the boy himself. They all just wanted to keep *her* safe, like they'd do for any of their pack mates.

The sound of Mathilda's tires crunching on the gravel driveway echoed down the hall, pulling Ally out of her reverie. Before she could ask her tiny charge what he wanted to do, he spoke up.

"Hey Ally? Ally?" Charlie tugged on her shirt until her attention was on him. "I don't think that guy was very smart."

"What guy?"

"The man who took me," Charlie spoke, as if he was talking about someone who *hadn't* tried to kill him.

Ally struggled not to show any emotion, even though her anxiety shot through the roof. "Why do you say that?"

Charlie squinched up his face, thinking hard about his

answer. "It was kinda like he's never been around a pup before. He never even shifted to his wolf. I did though, and he couldn't catch me." His little chest puffed up with pride before his face fell. "But I got tired, and I was so scared and then I kinda tripped."

He looked so ashamed that Ally's heart broke a little. "It's okay, Charlie. You fought really hard. You were very brave."

The encouragement helped him smile again. "I *did* fight! When he finally got me, I bit him so hard he said words Mama won't allow me to repeat."

"Good for you!" She leaned in and whispered. "Were they the good ones?"

Charlie nodded. "I didn't know some of them and when I told them to Mama, her face got all red. I was lucky I was sick otherwise I would have gotten in *biiig* trouble."

"You are lucky indeed."

He shrugged, his expression changing from sunshine to rain in a split second. "I'm still mad he caught me. At school, I'm always the fastest in tag."

"I bet," Ally said, leaning back against the bed's footboard. She had the sense Charlie was about to launch into one of his epic chatting sessions.

"I'm actually good at all my schooling. I know my ABCs, wanna hear?"

"That's okay, I'm already pretty familiar with the alphabet."

"Do you know math? Because I'm *really* good at adding."

"What about subtracting?"

His gaze darted away, and his mouth twisted into a grimace. When he thought of something else he was good at, he snapped his attention back to her. "I'm also really good at shifting. Better than Lucy even, and she's a grown-up! Sometimes when she shifts back to human, she still has her tail!"

They giggled together over that, and Ally couldn't wait to tease her friend. She remembered having the same problem all too well during her early days as a wolf. Except when she'd done it, Brian had smacked her for being so stupid. Shaking the memory away, she changed topics.

"I know something else you're good at," she said, poking his nose.

His eyes grew wide and then crossed as he watched her finger, then he grinned up at her. "Crossing my eyes?"

"No, silly. At taking care of Ghost Kitty."

His smile faltered, then fell until his lower lip pooched out. "Papa won't let me keep all the kittens, even though I'm the one who saved them from burning up when that crazy man burned down Lucy's house."

Ally shook her head with exaggerated remorse. "So unfair."

"I know! He says it's my responsibility to find homes for them all, where they can live long and happy lives." His eyes went wide with the spark of an idea. "You and Kade should take one home! You're so nice and they deserve nice homes, don't you think?"

The kid was a natural born salesman. Ally managed to avoid giving an answer—she naturally gravitated to dogs, but Ghosty's kittens *were* pretty freaking adorable — and let Charlie ramble on about each individual kitten's unique traits and funniest habits. She laughed right along with him as he described them slipping and sliding all over the hardwood floors, play fighting with each other until they crumpled into a mass of purring fur, and their penchant for climbing Mason. Each chuckle lightened the load of guilt she'd been bearing.

After what seemed like minutes, but was probably closer to an hour, Ally heard Mathilda's tires crunching on the gravel again. That and Charlie's deep yawn were her cues that their visit had come to an end.

"Thanks so much for letting me visit, Charlie." She tucked him in.

His eyes drooped as he snuggled under the covers, then they shot open wide. "Will you take care of Ghost Kitty and the kittens while I'm sick? *Please?*"

As if to punctuate his request, the critters in question rounded the corner and clambered onto the bed. Each kitten curled into Charlie, effectively outlining his entire body, then Ghosty snuggled again his head. It didn't look as if he needed any help, but no one in their right might could say no to his pleading, worried face.

"Sure, champ. You get some sleep now, okay?"

He mumbled something that sounded vaguely like "okay", then cuddled up to Ghosty and promptly started snoring. Poor thing was wiped out and she couldn't blame him. She remembered quite vividly how exhausted she'd been after her own ordeal. At least Charlie had a loving pack to care for him.

Ally stepped lightly to the door—even though a nuclear blast probably wouldn't have woken the kid—and left it ajar as she headed down to greet Mathilda. Now that Charlie had forgiven her, she stepped lighter. Hell, she *felt* lighter. A load had been lifted, that much was certain.

The click-clack of claws drew her attention. Ghost Kitty trotted along behind her, but thankfully the brood of kittens must have been as tired as Charlie. Recalling the cat's Houdini-like instincts, Ally hatched a game plan. The last thing she wanted to do was chase the cat around the yard while Mathilda laughed her ass off. Not that she would, being an Omega and all, but still... Not a great first impression to make.

"Back, Ghosty," she muttered, nudging the cat with one foot as she reached for the doorknob.

She cracked the door open just enough to warn Mathilda to be careful, but it wasn't the Omega who stood on the other side. It took a moment for her brain to process what she saw. A tall, gaunt man with a scruffy beard and piercing pale green eyes. Then the aroma of rotting oranges and wet dog hit her nose and her blood ran cold.

"Brian."

CHAPTER TWENTY-TWO

THE HUNT FOR BRIAN HAD ONLY BEEN UNDERWAY FOR ABOUT ten minutes when Kade's phone buzzed, calling him back to the scene of the crime. They'd agreed to start the hunt in human form, so they might spot any small clues their wolves might overlook. If they found nothing, they'd shift and let their noses lead the way. Except they'd barely got started!

Gritting his teeth and balling up his fists, he tramped through the forest, hoping one of them had finally found something that might lead them to the bastard. Otherwise, every second they weren't searching was another second lost.

When he reached the clearing, Mason, Gavin and about a dozen sentries stood in a cluster at the base of the tree Charlie had been chained to. Whatever was going on, their grim expressions hinted that it wasn't good news.

"What's up?" Kade asked.

Mason frowned, gesturing with his phone. "Just got word from the National Ruling Circle."

"Why'd you get them involved?" Kade tried to keep the growl out of his voice. "This is our turf, our problem, not theirs."

"And Brian Riverson is a criminal at large," Mason shot back. "I have a duty to report to the National Ruling Circle, you know that."

Kade rolled his eyes and shoved his hands into his pockets. "Well? What'd they say?"

Mason heaved a sigh. "They're sending a few of their own sentries out to help us hunt and capture Brian."

The entire group growled in response.

"I know, I know," Mason said gruffly.

"We don't need them," Anders, one of the sentries, grumbled. "This asswipe hurt Ally and Charlie. They can't expect us to let that go. It's our right to avenge our pack members, not the Ruling Circle's."

Everyone rumbled their agreement.

"Do you know what?" Mason asked Anders, who looked confused. "We have no idea what Brian did to people or wolves outside our pack. If he changed Ally almost ten years ago, what else has he done in the meantime? Nothing good, I can promise you that."

Kade's wolf paced inside him, growing more impatient every second they stood here not looking for this monster. He didn't care what the NRC wanted — if he got the chance to kill Brian Riverson, he would take it. He'd happily accept whatever punishment the NRC gave him.

"Listen," Mason continued, his tone relaxed, but Kade caught the undercurrent of dominance. "The best thing we can do right now is find this guy before the NRC arrives. Got it?"

"And if he gets killed along the way, no big loss," Quinn, another sentry, added with a snarl.

Mason held up a hand. "We have direct orders to capture Brian, *not* to execute him."

"Bullshit," Colin grumbled.

"Ignoring an order like that would make us no better than the Riversons," Mason said, all hint of easy-goingness vanishing from his voice.

Kade's upper lip twitched as he held back a snarl. Intellectually, he knew his brother was right, but his heart was doing the talking now. He wanted to taste his enemy's blood on his tongue as he ripped his flesh away from the asshole's bones and watch as the light in the other man's eyes blinked out forever.

"Mason's right," Gavin said, drawing groans from his men. "Brian used to be my best friend. I know for a fact he'd rather die than be imprisoned for the rest of his life. He doesn't deserve a quick, merciful death. He deserves a long life, rotting away in a tiny cell."

A few of the sentries nodded, but Kade held his tongue.

"I still say if he dies along the way, good riddance," Anders said, glancing around for support.

"Nobody is to kill him," Mason growled, leaving no room for argument. "That's an order."

Kade was about to tell his brother exactly what he planned to do to Brian Riverson, orders or not, when a wave of fresh, desperate fear consumed him. Sniffing the air, he looked around to see what had set off his wolf. Maybe Brian was nearby—it was the only reason he could think of for reacting that way when he was surrounded by his pack.

"Kade, what's wrong?" Mason asked. "You look tense."

"I don't know. One second I was ready to rip out someone's throat, the next I felt some strange, disconnected fear. Like it was me, but not me, if that makes any sense."

A handful of the better-trained sentries immediately braced themselves and started sniffing the air for the enemy. Mason smiled and slapped a hand on Kade's shoulder.

"It's not you, it's Ally."

"What?" That made zero sense.

"It's one of the perks of the bond you share now. You can feel each other's emotions from a distance, especially intense ones."

It only took Kade about half a second to realize what it all meant. Ally was in trouble. And there was only one kind of trouble bothering them these days.

Without waiting for Mason's permission, Kade sprinted toward the pack house, shifting mid-stride. He barely broke stride as his clothes shredded off his body. When another rush of intense emotion blasted his senses, he pounded the ground as hard and fast as his four feet could go. Every inch of progress took a century, every full stride a millennium. He sensed the others gaining ground behind him, but the only sound he heard was the steady thrum of his heart beating faster with each step.

After an eternity, he finally rounded the pack house. Dust billowed up around him as he skidded to a stop in the front yard, his mind kicking into overdrive in an effort to process the scene before him.

He didn't need to recognize the strange man as Brian Riverson—his sickly scent gave him away. Ally—in her human form, no less—clung to his back, and kicked and bit and scratched, all while screaming in his ear. Brian spun around, trying to dislodge her, but when he reached back to grab her, Ghost Kitty moved in for the kill

The cat was a gray blur of teeth, razor sharp claws, and puffed-up fur as she latched on to Brian's crotch, drawing a high-pitched screech from the former Alpha. He released Ally to bat at the devil shredding his junk, which gave Ally better access to bite his ear.

Off.

A chunk of fleshy cartilage landed in a puff of dust near Kade's paws, snapping him out of his half-amused, half astounded stupor. The rest of the search party surrounded the tussling trio, leaving Brian no chance of escape, but he was too busy to notice.

The creak of a door opening drew Kade's attention. Charlie Tipton, still dressed in his dinosaur pajamas, hurried across the porch as fast as his wobbling little legs could carry him. He hadn't fully shifted, but his fangs had descended, and he snarled and snapped at the man who'd kidnapped him. The poor kid was trying to shift, no doubt to protect Ally—or more likely Ghost Kitty—but he was still far too weak to manage the feat.

Just as Kade moved to get Charlie to safety, Ally gasped. Kade spun around in time to see her turn her attention away from Brian just long enough for him to reach back and throw her to the ground. She landed flat on her back with a pained "Oomph!"

Kade's vision went red.

Head hung low, drool pattering into the dust at his feet, Kade stalked up to the man as he tried to dislodge Ghost Kitty. One warning snarl from Kade did the trick, sending Ghosty bolting up to the porch to stand in front of Charlie, back arched and fur standing on end.

Once free of his tormentors, Brian dropped his hands, allowing Kade to get a good look at him. Tall, but not as muscular as an Alpha should have been. Gaunt face, yellowing eyes, and a long, bleeding gash from his hairline to his chin, where Ally had split his skin in two.

She really was a hell of a woman.

A nasty smirk spread across Brian's ugly face as he shot a glance in her direction, without ever letting his attention waver from Kade.

"I should have known you'd eventually come crawling in the dirt to the fucking Blackwoods," he spat. "Trash attracts trash."

Kade slunk a step closer, upper lip pulled back and quivering as he tried to keep his wolf from attacking. Even after everything, he couldn't allow his wolf to kill the man. If he wanted any chance of tasting Brian's blood, the asshole would have to shift first.

Ally sat up and glared up at Brian. "You better watch your mouth, shit-for-brains."

"Ha! My mate goes running to the pack that destroyed my entire family and I'm not supposed to be upset? Haven't you done enough to me already?"

"I'm not your mate," she snapped. "Never was. And you have a lot of nerve talking about what *I've* done to *you.*"

"What the fuck are you talking about?"

Brian took a step toward Ally and Kade snapped his jaws in warning. Brian barely noticed.

"Bitch, I made you! You're a powerful wolf because of me. No matter what you do or where you go, I'm always going to be part of you."

Ally laughed bitterly. "Bullshit! You ruined me. *I* made myself what I am today. A Blackwood."

The sentries that surrounded them took two steps closer, baring their teeth to show Brain exactly what would happen if he messed with one of their own. Instead of being intimidated, Brian let out a truly maniacal laugh.

"I'll kill every last one of them! And if you're lucky, I'll let you watch."

Ally growled at him, showing her fangs.

"And maybe I'll start with your biggest defender."

Kade braced himself for the attack. Brian would shift and lunge at Kade, which would give him the perfect excuse and opportunity to live out his fantasy to rip out the asshole's throat. But the moment Brian's paws touched the ground, he lurched away from Kade and right toward Charlie. Defenseless, half-crazed Charlie, who still stood on the porch trying his hardest to shift.

"No!" Ally cried as she brought her wolf forward.

Even if she was the fastest shifter on the planet, she would have been too late to save Charlie. Kade tore after the mangy, sandy-furred wolf, only a step behind. Brian was within feet of Charlie when Kade mustered every ounce of energy and strength he had and launched himself.

He almost overshot, but at the last second, he buried his claws into Brian's hide and his teeth clamped down on Brian's mutilated ear. They tumbled onto the stairs, a few inches from Charlie's feet, and finally landed in the dirt.

Dust choked Kade, but he ignored the minor discomfort to focus on keeping Brian from either Charlie or Ally. Each time the sandy wolf lunged toward the porch, Kade clamped his jaws hard on one exposed body part or another. Soon Brian's wolf was streaked with his own blood, but that didn't slow him down much.

Eyes darting between Ally and Charlie, the beast clearly was preparing himself for his final attack, one that Kade had no doubt would be swift and vicious. The wolf had no soul, so playing dirty came naturally to him. Kade was ready for anything, including a feint, then a quick change in direction. And that was exactly what happened, only not the direction Kade had expected.

Brian jerked toward Charlie once more, so Kade pushed off toward Ally. Then Brian was on him, fangs buried deep in the back of his neck. Kade became vaguely aware of Ally's frantic snarls, but he knew Mason would hold her back.

Dropping to the ground, Kade rolled onto his back, dislodging his opponent, but as quickly as he fell away, he was back again, this time pinning Kade to the ground. Kade could barely breathe from the foul stench of Brian's breath, but he managed to get his hind legs between him and Brian, so he could kick at his exposed underbelly. The only problem was that Brian's dripping fangs were mere inches from Kade's neck, and the insanity that blazed behind his eyes only grew stronger.

Brian went wild, gnashing his teeth and slobbering all over as he tried to reach Kade's throat. It didn't take an empathetic Omega to see Brian was fantasizing about how sweet it would be to take Ally's mate away from her before her very eyes before he killed her, once and for all.

If Kade had been fighting for anything but love for his mate, he could easily have perished under the onslaught. Brian had never loved anyone, so he had no conception of the power the fated mate bond offered. Kade's entire existence now was to protect and care for his mate, and he couldn't do either if he was dead, so his only option was to not only survive, but to *win*.

Kade channeled all the love he had for Ally to his feet, and with one powerful kick, threw Brian over his head and flat onto his back, knocking the wind out of him. He lay stunned long enough for Kade to scramble to his feet and loom over the deranged prick. As Brian lay gasping to fill his lungs, Kade didn't waste a second clamping his jaws on the wolf's neck.

Just a tiny bit more pressure and Brian Riverson would never get the chance to hurt anyone else ever again.

CHAPTER TWENTY-THREE

ALLY STOOD CRADLED IN KADE'S ARMS AS THEY WATCHED Gavin and his sentries drag Brian away. A small, vengeful part of her wished Kade had finished off the asshole who'd turned her life upside down and inside out, but a bigger, more loving part of her admired his restraint. No one would have blamed him for protecting his mate and pack mates, but he had chosen the high road, which only endeared him to her even more — if that was even possible.

"The RNC sentries will be here soon," he murmured in her ear, sending chills of love and lust through her body. "Then you'll never have to think about Brian Riverson again."

Mason had explained that the RNC would, at the very least, sentence Brian to life in prison for all that he'd done. If more came out during the investigation, he might get off easy with the death penalty. That spiteful part of herself hoped he'd skate by with life, because knowing he was suffering every day for the rest of his life lifted her spirits—and she didn't feel an ounce of guilt over it.

For the first time in nearly a decade, Ally could breathe again. A weight the size of the world had lifted from her shoulders and she felt something she'd never dared hoped she would feel again—*freedom!* She could finally step out of the shadows and embrace the light. Her life would be full of happiness and sorrow, joy and loss, excitement and fear. In other words, a normal life.

With Kade.

Spinning in his arms, Ally buried her face in her mate's bare chest and started sobbing. His scent changed from tired and satisfied to alert and confused. He pushed her to arm's length and searched her face.

"You said you weren't hurt. What's wrong?"

"Nothing, these are happy tears. I didn't realize it was all bottled up so tightly, and now it's coming out."

He twisted her arms to check for injuries anyway, then let his gaze slide down the length of her naked body and back up before taking her right hand in his. Examining her scuffed knuckles from when she'd punched Brian, he raised her hand to his lips and pressed a gentle kiss on the bruises.

"I've never seen knuckles so busted up. You really must hit like a girl."

"I'll show you who hits like a girl!" Ally feigned outrage and lightly punched his arm, even though she could probably hit him with all her might and it would still feel like a fly to him.

"You do," he said, laughing.

Apparently, Ghost Kitty didn't get the joke. In a blur of gray, she went from sitting at Ally's feet to hurtling toward Kade's crotch, just as she had with Brian. Kade shouted and jumped away before Ghosty could dig her claws in.

"Hey!" he shouted, moving Ally between himself and the protective cat. "Not all dangly bits are cat toys, you little monster!"

"Ooh, my protector," Ally teased as she kneeled to let Ghost Kitty jump into her arms for a cuddle. "Big scary wolf is afraid of an itty, bitty kitty."

Several of the remaining sentries and a handful of other pack mates chuckled at the scene, including Mason. He stomped up the porch steps and slapped his brother on the back.

"Looks like you're in a bit of trouble, little brother."

Keeping one suspicious eye on Mason and the other on the sharp-clawed cat, Kade asked, "Why?"

Mason nodded to Ally. "They've bonded."

"So?"

"*So,* you are now the proud owner of Ghost Kitty and six kittens."

"Wait just a min—"

"Who could be better protectors than a half-feral cat and her pack of mewling pussies?"

Kade mumbled something.

"What was that?" Mason asked."

"Glaring," Kade spat out, looking defeated. "A group of cats is called a glaring."

Ally laughed, then turned pleading, batting eyes on her mate. *Pleeease,* she begged mentally.

Kade rolled his eyes and released a long, irritated growl. "Dammit."

Mason roared with laughter as he joined his men again, leaving Ally to approach her mate, the last of her tears drying on her smiling cheeks.

"Come on, Kade. Having a house full of cats will be fun." She raised one of Ghosty's paws in the air and gave it a high-five. "See? She can even do tricks."

Satisfied that Ally was no longer in immediate danger, and no doubt annoyed at being manhandled, the cat leaped down and sauntered away in search of her kittens. Once she'd rounded the corner, Kade pulled Ally into his arms again and kissed the tip of her nose.

"It's a good thing for that damn cat that I love you so much and want to make you happy. Otherwise she and all her demon spawn would be right back out on the street."

Ally grinned up at him and brushed a strand of hair away from his brow. "Know what else would make me happy?"

"I know what would make *me* happy right now," he said quietly, waggling his eyebrows.

Ally smiled, then grew earnest. "No, seriously. I want to go to Alabama to see my family again. I hate that they've thought I've been dead all this time, but it was the only way I could come up with to protect them. If they'd known I was alive and, on the run, they wouldn't have stopped searching for me. It might have drawn Brian's attention. I can't tell you how much I've missed—"

She broke off, biting back the renewed threat of tears.

Kade nodded. "I figured that would be high on your to-do list. We'll go visit as soon as things calm down. And of course, once we have news to tell them."

"You don't think the news I'm alive is going to be enough?"

"Well, you're okay and everything," he teased, a glint of mischief in his eye. "But imagine how happy they'll be when they find out they have a grandbaby on the way too?"

Ally blinked in surprise. "Wow, you move fast."

"Always." He kissed her cheek. "But try to tell me you don't want it, a mini-you. Even better, a mini-me."

She knew he was joking, but Ally didn't laugh. "The world would be a much better place with more men like you in it. I love you so much, Kade."

"So, is that a yes?"

"No, it's a 'Hell yes!'" Taking his hand, she led him down the steps and around the corner, toward their cabin. "In fact, let's start trying right now."

EPILOGUE

Heat shimmered off the white sand as Gavin trudged across the beach, slacks rolled up, dress shoes in hand and his suit jacket slung over his shoulder. He'd sweated through his shirt the second he stepped out of the air-conditioned offices of the National Ruling Circle, he didn't want to ruin his jacket too.

Peering through the rolling waves, he could just make out the back of Mason's head at water's edge. That meant the blondish blob had to be Lucy and the brownish one was Ally. Kade was probably in the water. Gavin tried not to feel bitter that they'd been having a lovely beach vacation, while he'd been stuck indoors all damn day. His only consolation was that the beach offered a fantastic view— of the ocean *and* of scantily clad ladies frolicking in the waves.

"How was the meeting?" Mason asked when Gavin dropped to the towel next to a sunbathing Lucy.

"As if you don't already know," Gavin shot back

Mason offered a half-hearted shrug. He'd obviously planned the mini-vacay the minute he'd learned the NRC wanted Gavin to travel to Ft. Lauderdale for a meeting. Gavin had tried to get it out of his brother what they wanted, but Mason had feigned ignorance. Maybe he'd been ordered to stay quiet, or maybe he just liked tormenting his youngest brother.

Gavin huffed and glared out at the placid ocean. Under different circumstances, he might have enjoyed a trip to the beach, but his meeting with the National Alpha, Beta and Enforcer had soured his mood.

"I still don't understand why you all had to tag along," he grumbled.

Lucy rolled onto her side and lowered her sunglasses a smidge. "And miss out on a vacation in Florida? Yeah, no. I can't afford to pass up some fun in the sun. I'm going to start showing soon, and after the pup comes…"

She rubbed her belly, where the future of the Blackwood rested.

"What's your excuse?" he asked Ally as Kade jogged up, dripping in seawater.

She glanced up at her mate and raised a questioning

eyebrow. He smiled, then shook his head like a dog, spraying them all with water. The women squealed, and Gavin glared. He'd been trying to not get his one and only suit too dirty.

"What was that look?" Lucy asked, excitement lighting her face.

Ally blushed. "Nothing's certain yet, but Mathilda said she sensed *something* growing in me."

Lucy squealed again and pulled her friend into a tight hug. Kade flopped down next to his mate and laid a protective hand on her stomach.

"I keep telling her it could be some crazy alien that's going to eventually eat its way out—"

"Enough!" Ally scolded, though it held little weight since she was grinning at the same time. "You will not talk about our child that way."

"Sorry, my love." He leaned forward and kissed the tip of her nose, then turned his attention to Gavin. "So, what'd I miss? What was the meeting about?"

Gavin frowned. "Roman wants me to head up the relocation process for the rest of the Riverson pack, if you can call it that."

"I thought they all bolted as soon as they'd heard Brian had been caught," Kade said.

"Apparently not. I guess Brian's Beta, some guy named Paul Gibson, managed to escape with some other higher-ups before the NRC sentries caught up with the pack. They took a handful of the worst wolves into custody, and it sounds as if they're pretty keen to spill their guts."

"No kidding?" Ally asked as she rubbed sunscreen on her arms.

"One of them was Brian's enforcer. He got pretty chatty once they offered him a deal to release him from prison sometime in his late sixties. Guess he thought that sounded better than dying in a cage. They've already caught a couple of the fugitives thanks to his blabbing, and they're hoping for even more."

"And so, ends the saga of the Riverson pack," Lucy said, lying down and putting her shades back in place.

"Not really," Gavin said. "It's really only half the battle. Unfortunately, a good number of otherwise normal wolves wound up members of the pack, too. Brian's enforcer told Dane, the NRC Enforcer, they'd been running a sort of racket of false promises to grow the pack. Once they were in…"

"They couldn't get out," Ally finished for him, nodding sadly.

"Exactly," Gavin said. "Now they don't even have the promise of a pack."

"I've already agreed to take on anyone who wants to join us," Mason said.

"That's what Roman said. He also said I was the perfect choice to process all those wolves and find alternate packs for those who don't want to join us."

"Why wouldn't they want to join us?" Lucy asked. "We're awesome!"

"Agreed," Kade said.

Ally veered the conversation back on topic. "Where are they all now?"

"Tessa's house in Pepper," Lucy answered. "It's not much, but it's better than wandering around the woods, lost and afraid."

Ally whistled, worry etching her brow. "Crap, even if the pack hasn't grown since I escaped, that's still a lot of people to be living in such a cramped space. They're already under a ton of stress, I can't imagine they're going to have much fun packed in there like sardines."

Gavin scrubbed a hand over his face. "Yeah, it's going to be a big job."

"Sounds like you've got a lot of work ahead of you, little brother," Kade said.

Mason popped a beer and took a sip before letting out a

refreshed sigh. "Well, what are you waiting for? Better get started."

He jerked his head back toward the hotel. Gavin balked as he watched a beautiful young woman jog by in a bikini top and a thong.

"You've got to be kidding me! You ride my coattails to get a vacation and then you're not even going to let me enjoy the beach bunnies for an afternoon?"

Mason smirked. "Them's the breaks. Now get to work."

IF YOU ENJOYED THIS BOOK, PLEASE BE TOTALLY awesomesauce and leave a review so others may discover it as well. Long review or short, your opinion will help other readers make future purchasing decisions. So, go forth and rate our level-o-awesome!

Check out book #3 in the Real Men Shift series: Real Men Growl

Buy or Borrow at Amazon

Dust tickled Gavin's nose until he lingered at the terrible edge of nearly sneezing… only for it to vanish, leaving him tense with anticipation. Now he wanted to sneeze but couldn't. The closest thing he could compare the experience to was losing out on an orgasm before sliding into home plate. Not that he'd ever experienced such a tragedy. Nope, not him. That kind of thing didn't happen to the youngest Blackwood brother—and enforcer of the Blackwood pack.

Not that he'd done much enforcing lately.

The National Ruling Circle had entrusted Gavin with handling the merging of Brian Riverson's hodgepodge pack with others, though a good number of them were moving to Blackwood. With the lunatic in custody, the ex-alpha couldn't stand in the way. Brian's crazier father, Frank, was dead and was no longer a concrete block in the way, either.

Unfortunately, the damned transition was made doubly difficult due to Riverson's half-assed, confusing as hell bookkeeping. *Did they even know how to add and subtract? What the hell?*

Gavin had been in tiny Burrman, Georgia, for days—most of it in Brian's small office tucked in the far corner of the pack house. He'd been hunched over the desk, scouring what few records he could find to try and untangle the mess. Mostly what he'd discovered were the rantings of the certifiably insane.

And Post-its. So many damned Post-its plastered over just about every flat surface available. As far as he could tell, none had any real value or meaning. He'd kept only one, which depicted a giant robot shooting laser beams from its eyes. It seemed to sum up the Riversons' philosophy on pack leadership perfectly.

Rubbing his nose frantically to rid himself of that itchy, unfulfilled remnant of a failed sneeze, Gavin pulled open the bottom drawer of Brian's desk. He'd already checked every nook and cranny in the cluttered and utterly disorganized office twice. Yet he still hadn't found the pack registry documenting births, deaths, desertions, and any other major event of note within the pack. It had to be hidden in there somewhere, but the place was such a mess, it might take weeks to sniff out its hidey hole. Weeks he sure as hell didn't want to spend in Burrman.

Instead of rifling through the junk in the drawer—again—Gavin pulled out the entire thing and set it on the desk. It still held the same contents as the last two times he'd peered inside: a handful of ancient invoices, an empty bottle of Mad Dog 20/20—how poetic—a recipe book on how to cook on a cast iron stove, and a Celebration Barbie, of all things.

He was nearly ready to throw the drawer across the room when something odd about it niggled his mind. Something... not quite right. From the side, it appeared fairly deep, except the meager contents filled it to the top. He dumped the odd assortment on the desk and then returned the drawer to the surface of the desk. Now free of its contents, he reached in and tapped a knuckle on the drawer bottom. Just a couple of quick raps were enough to tell him the truth—the drawer had a hollow bottom.

Gavin ran his fingers along the edges, and the tips just glanced over the edge of a tab that stuck up between the bottom and side. He hadn't seen it in the past, but now that he knew it was there, the small piece was obvious. Except his man-fingers couldn't grasp the tiny bit. He grumbled and growled when he realized he'd need help. To crack open a drawer. He mentally sighed and then drew in a deep breath.

"Nora!" he shouted toward the door.

Nora Cooper, a petite brunette in her early forties with piercing blue eyes and a pretty smile, had been serving as Gavin's assistant and liaison between him and the Riverson pack. Actually, he had to get out of the habit of referring to the wolves as Riversons. They'd unanimously voted to revert to their old name—Fields. And that vote had given him hope for the battered and bruised group of wolves. If they hated the name Riverson so much that they'd rename themselves, integrating into new packs might go smoother.

"You bellowed?" Nora poked her head around the corner.

Nora's lineage traced all the way back to the beginning of the Fields pack, and if the she-wolf didn't know someone —dead or alive—she knew *of* them. Gavin's job would have been ten times more taxing if Nora hadn't been around to help him.

"This drawer has a false bottom, but I can't get at the little tab thingy."

Nora's eyebrow shot up. "Tab thingy?"

Gavin grunted. "Dammit, just come and look."

Nora dropped her gaze and scurried toward him, her stare not going higher than the drawer on the desk. Fuck him sideways, now he wanted to kick his own ass. When he'd first arrived, she'd been meek as a mouse—not speaking unless spoken to and eyes practically glued to the floor. But as they'd worked together, she'd grown more comfortable with him, teasing him when he deserved it and even occasionally meeting his gaze. At least until he sounded the slightest bit gruff. Then she retreated into herself, hiding beneath that beaten shell for safety.

Gavin couldn't blame her, but he hated that Brian Riverson—and his father before him—had traumatized the pack so deeply. He hated that his behavior pushed them back to that place even more.

"Oh, I see it." Her breath caught, and she lifted her head slightly—just enough so he saw the excitement in her eyes.

Pinching the edge of the tab with her fingernails, she tugged gently until the bottom lifted free. Inside lay a large leather-bound record book covered with a thick layer of dust. Clearly Brian and Frank had been too busy mad-dogging to notice the drawer contained more than junk.

"What's this?" Gavin carefully lifted the book. He held it at an angle and blew a puff of breath across the cover. Dust filled the air in a cloud of pale grey smoke and just like that, the sneeze that'd been taunting him exploded from his nose. Nora squeaked and jumped. Then she snickered into her hand.

Gavin simply grinned, relief over Nora bouncing back after his growling rushing through him as quickly as his sneeze. He'd already learned that commenting on her quick recovery didn't lead anywhere good, so he refocused on the dusty journal they'd discovered. He placed it on the desk and flipped it open, the old cover releasing a slight creak as it moved.

The first page was filled with precise, blocky writing, almost as if every letter had been drawn with a stencil— not at all like the jagged, spikey letters he'd learned belonged to Brian Riverson.

"Whose handwriting is this?" He spun the book so Nora had a good view, watching as she flicked through a few pages and then released a mournful sigh.

"Well, I'll be damned," she breathed. "That's Alpha Fields' handwriting. I'd recognize it anywhere." She thumbed past a few more sheets. "It doesn't look as if Brian or Frank ever recorded anything."

Fields had been the alpha before being viciously murdered and overthrown by Frank Riverson. The death of their alpha had shaken the pack to its core, but with nowhere else to go, they'd remained in place to suffer under the Riverson name.

Concern washed over Gavin and he shot Nora a look, doing his best to sort through the scents around him—to gauge her emotions. She'd witnessed everything Frank and his mate had done and then all the evils Brian had rained down on the pack. Normally the wrong tone alone sent her into emotional hiding, yet she still remained in place, her fierce determination humbling him.

Gavin grasped the book and carefully pulled it from her grip, catching her gaze with his own. "It's obviously Alpha Fields' registry. Are you okay to go through it for me?"

"Stop babying me," Nora huffed and dropped into the chair across from him, crossing one thin leg over the other after she sat. "I'm old enough to be your mother."

Gavin snorted. "Hardly. Maybe an aunt."

That earned him a dark glare. "Make that older sister and you have a deal."

Gavin laughed and shook his head. "Deal. Let's do this."

"Hang on." Nora snared a yellow pad and pen from the

desk and perched it on her lap. Then she gave him a pert nod. "Okay, shoot."

"Oh, good idea." He pulled his ratty Moleskine overflowing with chicken scratch notes from his back pocket and hunted for a blank page. Never hurt to double up just in case something happened to their original.

The book appeared to be part-journal, part-pack registry, the old alpha detailing additions, those who left and wolves that were expelled. Each entry was accompanied by a short paragraph describing the wolf in question, including physical traits, personality quirks, family members, and why they earned a spot in the book.

"He kept good notes," Gavin mused. "Every entry is dated."

Flipping forward, he found a list of current members on the last day of every year. He skipped ahead to the last list in the book and read the final journal entry, his gut clenching while a sense of foreboding flooded him.

Strange things happening lately. I've had to call the electric company three times because the alarms keep short circuiting and turning off. Jenny says I'm overreacting, but I think something else is going on here. Sentries are reporting new smells near our borders, as if another pack is nearby. Trying to keep Jenny calm, but I can't deny I'm concerned.

· · ·

IT WAS DATED THREE DAYS BEFORE FRANK RIVERSON HAD attacked.

Gritting his teeth to keep Nora from sensing his emotions, he turned the page and ran his finger over the names.

"Okay, how about we go over the last list of members, so we can get an idea of where everyone is now?"

"Sounds like a plan, boss."

He flipped to a clean page in his notebook and wrote down the first name as he read it aloud. "Greg Johnson."

"Died just after that registry was taken. Natural causes."

"Julia Mables."

"Found a mate in another pack and moved."

"Dottie Mables."

"Julia's mother. Moved with her."

"Erica Fitzsimmons. Oh, I recognize her name. She's with Blackwood now."

Nora nodded.

Gavin read a few more names and allowed the knot in his chest to loosen. Maybe this wouldn't be so bad after all. Half the names had either relocated to Blackwood or found other packs. Healthy now. Presumably happy, in spite of their pasts.

"Gina Walter," he read, expecting to hear which pack she'd moved to.

Nora winced.

"What?" Gavin asked and then wanted to bite his tongue. He'd seen that look before.

She shook her head. "Gina is…dead. One of Brian's first victims, after Alpha and Jenny Fields."

Gavin pressed his lips together until they hurt and then jotted *Deceased, killed by Brian Riverson* in his notebook.

He took a deep breath and then read, "Sam Walter."

"Sam was Gina's mate," Nora said quietly. "They were young, early twenties. Newly mated. Once they killed her, they killed him too."

Nora swallowed hard. She was holding something back. Gavin remained silent, waiting for her to fill him in.

"I don't want to upset you with these details, Gavin, but you should note them. For the trial."

Gavin nodded. "It's okay, Nora."

"They didn't just kill Gina. They raped her first. And they made Sam watch."

Gavin's jaw cracked, but he kept tight hold on his emotions for Nora's sake as he scribbled in his notebook. "Okay."

The next few names went by without incident, but he didn't dare get his hopes up that the hard part was over. He'd heard enough about Brian to know the worst was yet to come. Sure enough, a handful of names later, more horror at the hands of the madman. And so, it went for far too long, the ebb and flow of tragedy and the people who'd survived, pausing only to regroup from the truly terrible cases.

Ones like Devon Lucas, who'd mouthed off to his new alpha and had been "taught a lesson"—chased through the forest until he was captured and torn to shreds. Or David Foster who had been murdered when he'd objected to one of Brian's enforcers taking his teenage daughter as a mate against her will. Then the eventual death of the girl when she tried to run.

The hate in Gavin's heart burned hotter with every detail Nora spat out, but he kept his composure. Or at least tried, until he reached the final name on the list.

"Eric Jasper Fields."

Nora's only response was silence. The air—already pungent with the scent of tension—turned briny and bitter with the smell of nerves, dread, and anxiety. Nora was on edge about this one. Taking yet another deep breath to control himself, he set down his pen and turned his full attention to her.

"What is it?"

She shook her head, but when no words came, he tried again in his most patient tone. "Tell me about Eric, Nora."

Nora chewed her bottom lip and avoided his gaze.

"Nora," he said a little more forcefully, allowing some dominance to leak past his strict control, despite not wanting to upset her.

Fear flashed in her eyes, which brought a fresh wave of shame to Gavin, but he needed to know what she hid about this Eric person. After a long moment of contemplation, and one very searching look from Nora, she took a deep breath and spoke.

"Eric was Alpha Fields' newborn son."

Was. Past tense. That brought the ugly feelings back into Gavin's gut. Brian Riverson was an asshole, everyone agreed on that point, but was he so grotesque as to murder an infant?

"Is the pup dead?" Gavin asked, his voice thick with emotion.

Nora lifted her eyebrows nearly to her hair. Her 'What the hell do you think?' didn't need to be said. "Eric was a half-breed pup. Alpha Fields mated with a human, and the baby couldn't shift."

"So?"

Lots of mixed pups couldn't shift right away, but they grew into it eventually. Nora rolled her eyes at him.

"So...do you really think Alpha Fields' non-shifting, half-breed pup would be welcome in the new alpha's pack house?"

A baby. What a miserable fucking excuse of a wolf. To murder an innocent baby... His wolf howled in rage and grief for the child he didn't even know. Gavin swallowed hard and then carefully closed the journal.

"Thank you, Nora. I think now's a good time to take a break."

Hatred seethed in his heart, and he barely noticed Nora's wariness when he strode past her and out the door. He ignored everything—the piles of garbage littering every corner of the pack house, as if some frat boys had held a rave the night before. Even though Brian had been arrested weeks earlier, they hadn't gotten around to the mess. He stripped off his shirt and quickened his pace. By the time he pushed through the back door, his fangs had descended.

There was too much horrible shit in this small part of his world for him to keep it all together. He needed to run, to rage against the evil that was Brian Riverson, to dig his claws into the dirt until his head and heart no longer ached.

"Anders! Quinn!"

The sentries were stationed just inside the tree line, on either side of the pack house. The leaves softly rustled when they darted out and joined their leader.

"You should already be running," he growled, his voice gravelly from the power of his wolf.

The men didn't need to be told twice. Breaking into a sprint, they tore their clothes off as they raced and then shifted into their wolf forms. Black fur sprouted along Gavin's spine, and his muscles twitched and contorted while his body lengthened. Once on all fours, he howled loud and proud, relieved to let his animal take control.

His men had already disappeared into the dense forest, so Gavin darted in after them, eager to chase them through the woods—and chase away the fury that had built inside him.

Brian Riverson was in the past. All of the suffering he'd doled out was in the past.

Now it was time for a little fun.

Buy or Borrow at Amazon

ABOUT THE AUTHORS

CELIA KYLE

Ex-dance teacher, former accountant and erstwhile collectible doll salesperson, New York Times and USA Today bestselling author Celia Kyle now writes paranormal romances. It goes without saying that there's always a happily-ever-after for her characters, even if there are a few road bumps along the way. Today she lives in central Florida and writes full-time with the support of her loving husband and two finicky cats.

Website

Facebook

MARINA MADDIX

New York Times & USA Today Bestselling Author Marina Maddix is a romantic at heart, but hates closing the bedroom door on her readers. Her stories are sweet, with just enough spice to make your mother blush. She lives with her husband and cat near the Pacific Ocean, and loves to hear from her fans.

Website

Facebook

Printed in Great Britain
by Amazon